The Adventures Of

SASSY AND ROWDY

Episode 1

The Enchanted Valley

By Marvin E. Jones

Illustrated By

Tim Czarnecki

EAKIN PRESS ★ Austin, Texas

ISBN 0-89015-750-2

"Mother Will Build You a Rainbow" lyrics by Kevin Hard

Library of Congress Cataloging-in-Publication Data

Jones, Marvin E.
    The enchanted valley / by Marvin E. Jones : illustrated by Tim Czarnecki.
    p.   cm. — (The Adventures of Sassy and Rowdy Krackers : episode 1)
    Summary: Three human children and their raccoon friends encounter many
strange inhabitants of the Enchanted Valley and become involved in a quest to
rescue the raccoons' mother from her imprisonment.
    ISBN 0-89015-750-2 : $9.95
    [1. Raccoons — Fiction. 2. Fantasy.]   I. Czarnecki, Tim. ill.   II. Title.   III.
Series: Jones, Marvin E. Adventures of Sassy and Rowdy Krackers : episode 1.
PZ7.J7219En   1988
[Fic] — dc20   89-72181
                                                                            CIP
                                                                             AC

This book is dedicated to my loving children,
who are also my best friends:
Kenneth, Randy, Rickey,
Dennis, Tommy, Kevin, and Donna.

The Human Family

Uncle Jim

Pete

Kevin

Tommy

Donna

Samantha

Charles

Contents

Preface

Fairy tales, legends, and myths have entertained children throughout the ages. Families have joined together by candlelight while these tales unfolded fantasies in their minds.

The Adventures of Sassy and Rowdy series, dedicated to the entertainment of children, embraces modern times with fantasy and science fiction to promote wholesome family values. The entire story unfolds in three books: Episode 1, *The Enchanted Valley*; Episode 2, *Gory Gary Strikes Back*; and Episode 3, *Danger in the Big Thicket*.

It is hoped you will take time to join your family in reading them together. Enjoy the delightful experience of a family sharing love and laughter as you follow Rowdy and Sassy's adventures in the world of fantasy.

The Kracker Family

Sebastian

Sassy   Rowdy

Chapter 1

The Trap

Deep in the heart of Texas lies a vast wilderness known as the Big Thicket. Its beautiful forests and dense undergrowth are interwoven with flowing springs and waterfalls. Its beauty and splendor are matched only by its intrigue and mystery. It is here in this paradise of wildlife that we find the home of Sassy Krackers and her twin brother, Rowdy. They live comfortably and snugly in their hollowed-out home in the large old hickory tree.

Sassy is a sweet, loving little gray raccoon with large brown eyes. She is the sweetheart of all the animal kingdom of the Big Thicket. Rowdy is a mischievous brown raccoon who seems to be into everybody's hair. He is quite a bodacious and daring little fellow who loves pranks. One of his tricks is to replace Lady Jaybird's eggs with prickly pears and watch her squawk as she leaps from her nest when she sits on them. Both of these young raccoons live under the watchful eye of their father, Sebastian.

One fine spring day in the Big Thicket, the trees were budding out with leaves and everything was in bloom. Sebastian stretched out on the limb of the old hickory, soaking in the sun's warm rays, while his big bushy eyes searched the for-

1

est below for danger to Sassy and Rowdy. They were playing around the trunk of the old hickory tree.

The morning stillness was suddenly interrupted by Gizmo Crow, who swooped down sounding the latest news. "Sebastian," he squawked, "they're moving in."

"Who is moving in?" asked Sebastian.

"Well, didn't you hear?" replied Gizmo.

"No, I didn't hear," answered Sebastian with a little annoyance in his voice.

"Well," said Gizmo as he sat on the limb by Sebastian, "the old farm on the edge of our forest that has been abandoned for years . . ." Gizmo paused and lifted his claw to scratch his beak, then looked around.

Sebastian was becoming impatient for him to finish his story. "Well, get on with it. What about the old farm?"

"Oh, yes, yes," said Gizmo, "there is a human family moving into it."

"How many humans?" Sebastian asked.

"Well, there is a man, three children, a farmhand, and two dogs."

2

At this Sebastian leaped to his feet and exclaimed, "Dogs, you say! Dogs are trouble to the small animals of the forest." Sebastian paced anxiously up and down the limb for a moment, then asked Gizmo, "How big and what kind of dogs?"

"Well," replied Gizmo, "they're small dogs and seem very friendly."

Sebastian glanced quickly down at Sassy and Rowdy, still playing around the old hickory, then stared out into space as he reflected back on the loss of the young raccoons' mother. A tear slipped from the corner of his sad old eyes as he turned to Gizmo and said, "When Sassy and Rowdy were very small, their mother was chased by Hunter John's dogs into one of his traps. Hunter John came and carried her away and we haven't seen her since . . . We don't even know if she is still alive."

Sebastian leaned up against the trunk of the old hickory, then continued. "Gizmo, it is bad enough that we have to put up with Hunter John and his traps and those two vicious dogs of his, but now this new threat. Still another human family and their dogs. Perhaps I should move my family deeper into the forest."

Gizmo lifted his head, stretched his neck vigorously, then suggested, "Why don't we have Sheriff Dallas Possum investigate this family and see if they are hunters?"

"That's a good idea," replied Sebastian. "Go now, please, find Sheriff Dallas and send him to me." Gizmo jumped from the limb and flew away to search for the sheriff.

The morning breeze gently lifted Sebastian's fur as he gazed toward the old farm where the new human family was busy moving in. The head of this family was Uncle Jim, a small-town newspaper editor. Living with him were his two nephews, Tommy and Kevin, and their sister, Donna. Most of the work was being done by Pete, their farmhand. Their two small dogs, Charles, a black schnauzer, and Samantha, a reddish-brown cocker spaniel, were running around the old farmhouse, sniffing out their new surroundings.

"Uncle Jim," shouted Tommy, "may we go into the forest and play?"

"Yes," replied Uncle Jim, "but don't go out of shouting

3

distance, as you don't know this area very well."

The children took their two dogs and scrambled off down the hill toward the Big Thicket. They were filled with the excitement of a new adventure.

Meanwhile, Sassy and Rowdy had ventured quite a distance from the old hickory to play around Skull Waterfalls. They always found excellent swimming and fishing in the pool at the base of the waterfalls.

What the young raccoons didn't know was that there had been another visitor to the waterfalls earlier in the morning. Hunter John had set three cage traps thereabouts, hoping to catch some of the small animals as they came to the pool.

The sun's rays beamed through the tall trees as the wind blew the limbs about, causing the sunbeams to dance on the ground. Sassy and Rowdy hurried toward the pool. Suddenly, they heard a familiar voice in the tree above.

"Hi, Sassy. Whatcha doin', Rowdy?"

Scurrying down the big pine was Sparkie Squirrel.

Rowdy, holding a stick in his hand, pointed toward the waterfalls and said, "We're going swimming. You want to come along, Sparkie?"

Sparkie hit the ground and bounded up to them, saying in an excited tone, "Sure, why not? It's a great day! But keep your eyes open because I heard Hunter John's dogs, Spike and Otis, earlier today."

The three started out together toward Skull Waterfalls, laughing and playing leap frog, unaware of the loaded cage traps waiting for them.

Some distance away the human children were playing at the edge of the forest. Charles and Samantha left the kids to explore deeper into the forest.

Charles suddenly stopped. "Listen, Samantha, what do you hear?"

Samantha perked up her ears. "A roaring sound. Maybe we should return to the children."

"Nonsense," said Charles, "it's just water. Don't be such a chicken, Sam." Sam is what he called Samantha when he was annoyed with her. "Let's go take a look," he said. The two dogs moved deeper into the forest toward Skull Waterfalls.

Samantha's small bobbed tail began to wag back and forth very nervously as she said, "Charles, it sounds awfully frightening. Are you sure we should do this?"

Charles pranced along in front of her, his tail and head held high. "There is nothing to be afraid of except fear itself."

Samantha quickened her pace to stay close to him and answered, "I wish I had your confidence."

Sassy, Rowdy, and Sparkie were already playing about the pool. Sparkie and Sassy were taking turns dashing under the waterfalls while Rowdy remained on the other side of the pool. He was finding a special delight in throwing flat rocks across the top of the water, watching them skip and hop. He spotted a choice, round, flat stone just right to skip over the entire pool. Taking it firmly in his hand, he backed up to try a bounce off the edge of the bank and across the top of the water. With a super windup, he let it fly. To his disappointment, it overshot the bank and struck the top of a lily pad just inches out in the water.

"Ouch," cried a gruff voice from beneath the lily pad.

"Who's there?" shouted Rowdy.

"Just me," said Leaper Frog as he crawled up on the land.

"Whatcha doing hiding under the lily pad, Leaper?"

Rubbing the bump on his head, Leaper replied, "Just resting."

"Hey, Leaper," said Rowdy, "I have an idea for a great game. Do you want to play?"

"What kind of game?"

"Well, see that giant lily pad way out in the pool?"

"Yeah," said Leaper.

Rowdy eased over next to Leaper, put his arm around him, and said, "Leaper, you swim out and get on top of the lily pad and I will skip rocks by you and you can catch them."

"Oh, no, Rowdy, I can't do that."

"Why not?" asked Rowdy, placing his hands on his hips.

"Well," said Leaper, "I just can't."

Rowdy walked around Leaper, eyeing him up and down. "You afraid I'll hit you with one?"

"No, no," replied the frog, "that's not what I'm afraid of."

"Well," exclaimed Rowdy, "what are you afraid of?"

Leaper looked around carefully to see if anyone could hear, then replied, "Rowdy, if I tell you something very personal, can you keep it a secret?"

Rowdy's ears perked up and his eyes widened, expressing a special, boyish delight in obtaining a secret. He assured Leaper that he would keep the secret. The two of them climbed up on a log by the edge of the pool and the frog began to explain. "Rowdy, haven't you noticed that every time you come to the pool, I am always sitting on a log, or stone, or just at the edge of the water?" Rowdy looked at Leaper and nodded his head. Leaper continued, "Well, you see, the embarrassing truth is, I'm afraid of water."

Rowdy flipped off the log backwards, holding his belly and rolling on the ground, laughing. "You're kidding me, Leaper! A frog that's afraid of water! That's like a raccoon being afraid of a tree!"

Leaper turned around on the log and faced his friend, who was still rolling on the ground, and said, "Well, that may be so, but it's still the truth. I have been afraid of water ever since I can remember, and I wish there was something I could do to overcome my fear. Do you have any ideas?"

Leaper did not realize it was a mistake to ask the mischievous Rowdy if he had any ideas.

Rowdy, lying on his back on the ground, looked up at his friend and a little devilish grin spread across his face. He was getting a wonderful idea for a simply terrific prank he could play on his friend, the frog. Rowdy jumped to his feet. "Leaper, my friend, you have come to the right person."

Leaper's eyes lit up. "I have? You know something that will help me?"

Rowdy climbed back up on the log beside the frog and said, "Leaper, it just so happens that I have some magic pellets that will make you one with the earth."

The frog jumped off the log and hopped about a couple of times before replying, "Magic pellets, you say! There is no such thing as magic pellets to make me one with the earth. You're making fun of me."

"Oh, no," said Rowdy, "I am not making fun of you and

7

I really do have some pellets that will make you one with the earth. But if you don't want them, that's okay. I can always give them to someone else."

Leaper hopped about a few more times, looking at Rowdy with skepticism. Then he began to be unknowingly pulled into Rowdy's prank as he asked, "Where did you get these pellets and how do you know they will make me one with the earth?"

Rowdy slid off the log, walked over next to Leaper, and said, "That's another secret. But I do have them, and I promise you, they will make you one with the earth."

"Well," said Leaper, "give me a couple and I'll try 'em."

Rowdy slipped his hand into his pocket and pulled out a large box of BBs that he had found the day before by the old creek. He pulled a couple of them out and gave them to the frog.

Leaper quickly swallowed them, then looked at Rowdy. "I don't feel a thing."

"Well," replied Rowdy, "maybe you need to take a few more." Rowdy gave him five more and Leaper gulped them down. "Now," said Rowdy, "do you feel something?"

"Well," answered Leaper, "I do feel a little strange. But I still don't think they're working."

Rowdy said, "I know what the problem is. These pellets are for small critters and you're a large frog. You need to take the whole box." And with that statement, he pulled out Leaper's bottom lip and poured the remainder of the box into the frog's mouth. "Now swallow them," he said. The frog, struggling with the load of BBs in his mouth, finally managed to get them swallowed. "Now," said Rowdy, as he slapped his hands on his knees, "do you feel one with the earth?"

With a look of distress on his face, Leaper replied, "The only thing I feel is extremely heavy and — oh, I can't move! I can't hop!" The frog's eyes widened in terror. "You lied to me! You tricked me! Help! Help!" cried Leaper.

Rowdy, once again rolling on the ground with laughter, said, "I didn't lie to you, Leaper. I told you they would make you one with the earth, and they have done that! You can't move! You and the earth are one!"

Leaper, frantically trying to hop, yelled loudly for Sassy. She and Sparkie, hearing the frog's pleas for help, quickly scurried to his side.

"What is wrong, Leaper?" asked Sassy.

"Rowdy tricked me and poured me full of pellets, telling me they would make me one with the earth . . . and now I can't move."

Sassy reached down and took the frog by his hind legs, held him upside down, and began shaking the BBs out.

As the last pellet was shaken out, Sassy put Leaper down. The frog began to hop about in delight, saying, "Oh, thank you, thank you so much, Sassy." Leaper then hopped over to Rowdy and shook a webbed toe at him, saying in a rough voice, "Rowdy, if you don't stop playing pranks on the critters of the forest, the Who-Done-Gotcha monster is going to get you!"

"Oh," said Rowdy, "I don't believe in the Who-Done-Gotcha monster. I think he's just a figment of somebody's imagination."

"He be no figment," proclaimed a voice from the bushes

as out strolled the Armadillo brothers, Arvin and Marvin. These two colorful brothers were the carriers of all the Texas tales and legends in the Big Thicket.

Arvin continued, "I heerd tell he be ten feet tall, and is hairy all over and have two big, beady eyes and large, sharp teeth."

"Yes," said Marvin, "and tracks be seed a coupla weeks ago down by the old creek, by Chuckie Beaver. The beaver sayed they be two feet long."

Arvin then added, "Story be havin' it, he older than the forest and meaner than ten wildcats what have crawdads a pinchin' on their tails."

"Yeah," said Marvin, "I heerd him hollerin' in the night and I be tellin' you, it be makin' my scales curl up on end."

The two then strolled over to Sassy and said, "Good mornin', little darlin'. What be bringin' up the subject of the Who-Done-Gotcha monster anyhow?"

Sassy related what had just happened to Leaper.

Arvin turned to Rowdy and said, "You be playin' pranks on the critters of this forest! You'd better be mendin' your ways or you'll be meetin' the Who-Done-Gotcha, sure 'nuff."

All the noise and excitement attracted the attention of Charles and Samantha, who suddenly jumped out of the underbrush and came face to face with the other animals.

"Dogs!" screamed Sparkie as he climbed a nearby tree. Marvin and Arvin quickly scurried back into the brush and Leaper slipped into the water underneath his lily pad, leaving Sassy and Rowdy standing alone to face the dogs.

Rowdy, with his fur raised on his back and growling, said, "Quick, Sassy, let's run for the waterfalls."

Charles and Samantha, stunned for a second by the animals' fright, started to reassure them that they meant no harm. But the young raccoons had already whirled and were running through the underbrush toward the protection of the honeycombed holes about the waterfalls. In their haste, fleeing from what they believed to be danger from the dogs, their carelessness caused them to run headlong into one of Hunter John's cage traps hidden in the underbrush. Terror swept through the pair as they heard the awful sound of the cage falling about them.

Charles and Samantha quickly pursued the raccoons to explain that there was no need for fear. They found them trapped in the cage.

Sparkie had seen the entire event from the trees above. He began leaping from tree to tree until he was above the cage. He scurried down the trunk to within a safe distance and asked, "What are you going to do? Can you get out?"

Sassy replied, "Run fast, Sparkie! Get Papa! He will know what to do."

At that Sparkie hit the ground and headed toward the old hickory to tell Sebastian. Rowdy was lunging against the sides of the cage in a futile effort to get free.

Charles pranced about the cage and stated with some arrogance, "This is a fine mess you've gotten yourself into."

Rowdy, snarling and showing his teeth, turned quickly to face Charles, who was now peering in at him through the wire. "We wouldn't be in this mess if you hadn't chased us in here."

"My fine, little furry friend," replied Charles, with his head cocked back. "The fact of the matter is if you hadn't run, we would not have chased you. We only wanted to tell you that we meant you no harm. However, all of this is irrelevant at the moment. The only important issue is how to get you out."

With tears trickling down her cheeks, Sassy asked Charles, "You mean, you will help us?"

"Certainly, little lady."

Seeing all was safe, the Armadillos ventured back out of the bushes and joined the others at the cage.

Sassy once again addressed Charles, "How can we get out? I am so very frightened!"

Rowdy placed his arm about her and said, "Don't worry, Papa will be here soon. He will know how to get us out."

As if the little pair hadn't had enough trouble, there came the sound of still another threat.

As Samantha's ears popped up, she said, "What's that I hear?" The little band became quiet and listened.

Then the silence was broken by Arvin. "That be Hunter John's jeep and Spike and Otis be with him, we be hearin'." So it was. In the far distance they could hear the gears grinding and the roar of Hunter John's jeep.

"Oh, dear me," exclaimed Samantha, "who are Hunter John, Spike, and Otis?"

Rowdy, shaking a little, said, "He hunts the small animals of the Big Thicket with his traps and his mean dogs."

"Oh, dear, oh, dear," said Samantha, "I am small!"

Charles, now getting an idea in his mind, said, "Steady, Sam, I think I know how to spring this trap."

In the meantime Sparkie had reached the old hickory, where he found Sebastian talking with Sheriff Dallas. Sparkie shouted, "Sebastian, come quickly! Rowdy and Sassy are trapped in one of Hunter John's cages by Skull Waterfalls."

The two raced off together toward the waterfalls, Sebastian all the while remembering the terrible fate of his children's mother. His heart was pounding hard with fear. *I can't lose my children as I did their mother*, he thought to himself. He quickened his pace to get to their aid.

Back at the waterfalls, Charles was proceeding with his plan. "Not long ago I was lying on the floor listening to my

12

master, Jim, practicing a speech on opposition. He quoted some human scientist as concerning the law of levitation that went like this: 'Give me a pole long enough and a rock big enough and I can move the earth.' Well, using that principle, this cage top shouldn't be that hard to lift."

With that statement he then instructed the other animals to help him roll a large stone over by the cage. The two Armadillo brothers found him a long pole that was suitable. Just as they were about to place the end of it under the edge of the cage, Sebastian arrived. Upon seeing the two dogs, he immediately went into an attack mode, his fur standing straight up and his teeth bared.

Samantha, backing up and whining, said, "Oh, my gosh, he's going to attack us!"

Charles, proudly standing his ground, said to Sebastian, "Hold on, friend, we are here to help."

Sebastian, still in an attack mode, replied, "Help? You're dogs, and dogs don't help us. They hunt us. They are our enemies."

Charles pranced closer to Sebastian and, in a rather pompous manner, said, "My good fellow, that might be so in some cases, but let me remind you that the hunter and his dogs are drawing closer and we are here and we are trying to help. So I suggest that the logical thing to do is to put aside your distrust for the moment and help us free your children — unless you wish for them to be carried away."

At that moment Sassy cried out, "Papa, please listen to him. He is our friend and he is trying to help us. Hunter John is getting very close!"

With this plea from Sassy, Sebastian realized time was growing short and he must trust the dogs. He relaxed his attack mode. "How do you intend to free them?"

Charles quickly related the plan. The little band of animals gathered around, laid the pole across the stone, then placed one end of it under the edge of the cage. Then, all of them gathering at the other end, they pulled down with all their might on the end of the pole. To their amazement, the heavy cage gave way under the pressure and rose up enough so that Rowdy and Sassy could slip underneath the edge to freedom. Sebastian quickly grabbed both of his children and hugged and kissed them as he wept.

Samantha walked over and, laying her head on Charles' shoulder, sighed, "My hero!"

"Now, now," said Charles, "it was nothing. However, I estimate the enemy will be upon us in a couple of minutes, so I strongly urge that we do not tarry any longer here."

Sebastian agreed and said, "Come, my friends, and follow me. I know a place of safety."

So the little band of critters hurried away, leaving behind them the empty cage and a frustrated hunter and his dogs.

They reached a place of safety at the top of a high hill overlooking the pool and the waterfalls. There they rested. Sebastian later said to Charles and Samantha, "I am very sorry I misjudged your intentions and cannot thank you enough for your help. I will spread the word throughout the Big Thicket that you are our friends. Is there anything else I can do?"

"Well," replied Charles graciously, "you might remember that not all humans and all dogs are bad. We live with a human family that loves us and is kind to all animals." Sebastian nodded his head in a sign of understanding.

Sassy walked over and gave Charles a big hug. "You will always be my friend. I will watch for you in the forest so we may play together and have good times."

With that, Charles and Samantha said their goodbyes and left their new friends to return to the children still playing at the edge of the forest.

As Charles and Samantha trotted away, little did these animals know how much their love for each other would grow and how many exciting adventures they would have in the days to come.

Chapter 2

The Storm

Pete hurried about his chores on the old farm while he nervously watched the dark storm clouds banking in the west. He stopped occasionally to glance at the forest, where Kevin had gone earlier in the morning to gather some fresh berries. Pete had good reasons for his concern, as Kevin was long overdue and the storm clouds were growing darker and closer.

It was midday in the forest. The sun beamed straight down on Kevin as he sat by the bank of the old creek. His eyes watered as he looked around, trying to determine which way was home. He was hungry, so he reached his hand inside the pail of berries by his side and took a few to eat. A beautiful yellow butterfly lighted on the small bush beside him as he popped the berries into his mouth.

"Oh, little butterfly," he said, "I am hopelessly lost and I wish you could show me the way home." As he sat eating his berries and admiring the splendor of the graceful butterfly, his thoughts were suddenly interrupted by a strong gust of wind. The front edge of the storm was sweeping through the forest. Kevin leaped to his feet and looked at the dark clouds now rolling in overhead. *I'd better find my way out of here or at least find some shelter,* he thought. He started moving quickly along the

15

old creek bank, hoping it would cross under a road. Fear was beginning to show in his face as the winds grew stronger and the clouds blackened out the sun.

Sassy and Rowdy were scurrying toward their home in the old hickory when they saw Kevin. Sassy said, "Rowdy, that is one of the little boy children that Charles loves. It appears he is lost and afraid."

"Yeah," said Rowdy, "he sure looks frightened. Whatcha think we should do?"

Sassy replied, "Let's follow along close to him and make sure he doesn't get hurt." She then spotted another of her friends hurrying to his home. "Needles Porcupine," she shouted.

The porcupine, hearing her, turned and came over to the young raccoons. His quills were standing almost straight up in the wind. "Well, howdy," said Needles, "you trying to get home ahead of the storm?"

"We were," replied Sassy, "but now I need a favor from you."

"I'll be glad to do you a favor," answered Needles. "What do you need?"

"Well, I would like for you to go by the old hickory and tell Papa we're okay. Tell him one of the human children is lost and we are going to stay close to him and make sure he doesn't get hurt. Please tell Papa if the storm gets worse, not to worry. We will find shelter." Needles agreed and headed toward the old hickory.

Sassy and Rowdy began stalking Kevin, who was now starting to run. Large drops of rain began to fall as the storm winds grew more fierce and the clouds swirled in an evil blackness overhead. Kevin rounded a bend in the creek and spotted what was left of an old, half-torn-down shack. He thought, *What luck this is! This old shack will provide shelter*. He headed for it in a full burst of speed as the rain began to pour down. Sassy and Rowdy, now close behind him, also aimed for the old shack. The three arrived together and scurried inside.

Kevin, wiping the water from his face, noticed that the two young raccoons had followed him into the old shack.

"Well, little fellows," he said, "did you get caught in the storm too?"

Now, it is common knowledge in the Big Thicket that the critters have an understanding of the human language, but the poor humans have no understanding of the critter language. With this in mind, Kevin squatted down on the dirt floor and stretched out his hand toward the two little raccoons. Sassy and Rowdy, knowing the boy would not hurt them, came up and nestled their faces against his hand.

Meanwhile, back at the old farm, Uncle Jim had arrived home. Pete quickly told him that Kevin was caught out in the storm. Tommy, Donna, and the dogs took turns pacing the floor and looking out the window at the storm, which was now raging in full force.

Pete said to Uncle Jim, "I have lived in these parts for many years, and I can't remember a storm this bad."

Uncle Jim instructed Pete to stay with the children and if the storm grew worse to take them to safety in the cellar. "I'm going out to try to find Kevin," said Uncle Jim as he slipped on his raincoat. "I know Kevin is a very clever boy and he has probably found shelter, but I must try to find him anyway."

Samantha asked Charles, "Do you think he is okay?"

"I don't know," answered Charles, "but I am going with Master Jim to look for him." Charles continued, "Maybe some of the animals of the forest will help him."

Samantha sighed and said, "I hope so."

"Come, Charles," called Uncle Jim. As the two went out the door, Samantha looked longingly out the window after them as they disappeared into the storm.

In the meantime, at the shack, Kevin was making the best of the situation. He rummaged about the old one-room shack, pulled down some old curtains, and dried himself and the raccoons. Finding a dry spot in the corner, he sat down and cuddled the two little raccoons. They watched the storm raging outside through the east wall, which had fallen years before.

Kevin stroked Rowdy's head and declared, "Little fellow, I sure hope this old shack holds together."

The old creek was now swelling out of its banks as the

17

rain continued to pour down. Kevin leaned his head back against the wall and dozed off, with Sassy and Rowdy curled up on his lap.

At the farm, Pete paced the floor as he listened to the news broadcast on the radio. One of the small dams on the Great River had burst and was causing flash flooding on all the small creeks in the Big Thicket. The lights flickered and then went out in the old farmhouse as a wall of water knocked down power lines crossing the Big Thicket. Pete lighted a candle and whispered to himself, "Poor little Kevin, I hope you are all right."

Kevin, Sassy, and Rowdy were still napping in the old shack, unaware of the three-foot wall of water now coming down the old creek toward them.

Rowdy, the first to hear something, raised his head to listen harder. "Sassy," he cried, "wake up and listen." The two raccoons sat in Kevin's lap with ears perked up, listening as the roaring sound came closer.

Then, without further warning, the wall of water slammed into the side of the dilapidated old shack. The three remaining walls began to twist and burst apart. Rowdy, Sassy, and Kevin were swept up quickly by the raging waters. Tossing and tumbling, they were washed out into the main stream of the old creek.

Sassy and Rowdy, swimming fiercely beside each other, searched for Kevin. "There he is!" shouted Rowdy. Both young raccoons, fighting against the heavy current, swam toward Kevin. They watched the swift undercurrents jerking him beneath the water, then releasing him to resurface like a fishing bobber.

"He is going to drown," declared Sassy, "if we don't help him!"

Rowdy then saw the large door to the old shack coming toward them. "Quick," he yelled, "let's push this door over to the boy, then he can hold on to it." They grabbed the side of the door and, swimming and pushing with all their might, managed to get it within reaching distance of Kevin. The boy, seeing the door, grabbed the edge and pulled himself upon it. Sassy and Rowdy scrambled to join him on top of the old door.

This was quite a sight to behold! Three little companions on top of the large old door, hanging on for dear life, while being tossed about by the currents and swept faster and faster downstream.

Back on the farm, Uncle Jim and Charles were driven back in by the storm. They sat in silence in the house, waiting for the storm to break and clinging to the hope that Kevin was safe.

On the old creek the three were still using the door as a makeshift raft. They clung to it and each other. Rowdy and Sassy were concerned about Kevin, who was having trouble staying on. They held on to the raft with one paw and to the boy with the other. They seemed determined to see to it that he survived this ordeal, even at the risk of their own safety.

The swift currents of the old creek at last reached the Great River. The old door, turning and swirling, was swept out into the river. Now the three little buccaneers were about to begin an extraordinary adventure as they were carried down the Great River toward the Enchanted Valley.

Chapter 3

The Enchanted Valley

The rain had at last stopped. Kevin and his little raccoon companions, Sassy and Rowdy, were riding the old door as it swirled about in the Great River. The three were unaware that they were being watched as their raft approached the Giant Waterfalls that dump the Great River into the Enchanted Valley.

Willard, the Wizard Lizard of the Enchanted Valley, gazed into his large Oracle as it glowed amber. It projected the images of what was happening on the Great River.

Hanging upside down from the ceiling was Boo the Bat. Now, this was no ordinary bat, because unlike a regular bat, Boo had very good eyesight. Even though his eyes were crossed, they still served him quite well.

"Boo, come take a look," said Willard. Boo flew down and lighted on Willard's shoulder. "Do you see what is happening on the Great River?"

"Yes, yes," said Boo, "th-they are in a lot of t-trouble."

"That's right, Boo, but what else do you notice?"

"W-well," answered Boo, "th-they are going to be swept over the Giant Waterfalls and-and that will be the end of th-them."

"Boo," replied Willard, "that is not all I wanted you to see."

"It's n-not?"

"Look closer."

Boo rolled his crossed eyes around and focused quite intently on the images being projected by the Oracle. "Oh yes, yes . . . I see n-now what you m-mean."

"Yes," replied Willard, "the two small animals are more concerned for the boy's safety than they are for their own. This must be a remarkable human child to have such loyalty from the animal kingdom." Willard walked about the large Inner Chamber that housed the Oracle, then went on, "Boo, we have been forbidden by the Sagittarians to interfere in the affairs of the human family. Our prime directive is to watch over the Oracle and to be at peace with the animal kingdom."

Boo flew across and landed on the railing that surrounded the Oracle and asked, "M-Master Willard, y-you are going to do something about what is happening out there, r-right?"

"That's right," stated Willard. "Now go, Boo, and open that Outer Chamber and release the hidden door in the magnesium tree that protects the entranceway. Then wait for them at the entrance of the magnesium tree. I'm going to use the power of the Oracle to lift them off the river and transport them here. Bring them to me when they arrive."

Boo, astonished, argued, "B-but, Master Willard, n-no human has ever b-been inside our chambers, or-or seen the Oracle!"

Willard turned and gazed at Boo sternly. "Do as I tell you, Boo. I want a closer look at this boy. I have my reasons."

Boo, still unsure that Willard was doing the right thing, decided to present further argument against bringing a human inside the chambers. He leaped up on top of the Oracle and was about to proceed with his argument when Willard stretched out his finger and a sliver of electricity shot out and zapped Boo.

"Ouch-ouch!" yelled Boo, "I-I-I'm on my w-way!" Boo opened the Outer Chamber and released the hidden door in the magnesium tree, then clung upside down to the ceiling by the entrance to await their arrival.

Back on the Great River, Sassy, Rowdy, and Kevin now saw the Giant Waterfalls. They grasped each other and their raft, awaiting whatever their fate may be.

Willard leaned over, placed his hands on the Oracle, and concentrated on the images from the Great River. As the three approached the edge of the Giant Waterfalls, preparing for what they felt would be certain doom, they were astonished that the raft did not fall as it went over the edge. Instead, it floated through the air like a magic carpet.

"Great Jumpin' Jehoshaphats!" exclaimed Kevin as they sailed across the countryside. Rowdy and Sassy, still clinging to Kevin, secured a still tighter grip on each other as their eyes widened in amazement.

Soon the door began to lower slowly to the earth as Rowdy proclaimed, "Sassy, if I survive this, I promise I will never play another prank on any of the animals again!"

The door gently came to rest at the base of the magnesium tree. The three sat very still on the door for a few moments, looking at the open entranceway in the tree.

A very funny voice was heard coming out of the opening. "W-well, you gonna come in or-or just sit th-there?"

"Oh, Sassy," murmured Rowdy, "it's a Who-Done-Gotcha monster for sure!"

"I don't think so," replied Sassy. "Let's see if the boy goes in. If he does, we will."

Kevin slowly rose to his feet and ventured toward the opening, with Sassy and Rowdy following very closely behind him. Once all three were inside the opening, the magnesium tree closed behind them. Kevin looked around the walls that were now glowing with a dark-reddish tint. Sassy and Rowdy each had a firm grip on his pants legs.

Rowdy said, "Boy, quit shaking, you are frightening me."

Kevin looked down at Rowdy and replied, "I'm very sorry, I guess I'm a little frightened myself." Kevin's mouth flew open in astonishment and his eyes got big. He looked at Rowdy again and said, "Oh, my gosh, I heard you speak! We must have died in the waterfalls and gone to heaven!"

Sassy protested, "Don't say that! Now you're making me frightened."

"Oh-oh," said the funny voice, "n-now I'm getting scared t-too!"

"Who said that?" demanded Rowdy, jumping around with his fist doubled up.

"M-me," replied Boo.

The three frightened travelers looked up and saw Boo hanging upside down just above them.

"Who are you?" asked Kevin, still amazed he was talking with animals.

"Boo-Boo, that's who."

"Well, Boo-Boo, that still doesn't tell us much."

At that Boo flew down and sat on a small marble table in front of them. "It's-it's not Boo-Boo, it's just Boo. C-can't you speak a simple name?"

"I'm very sorry, Just Boo," replied Kevin.

"Y-you just can't seem t-to get it r-right! Why the Wizard would w-want to see y-you is more than I can understand. Y-you're not very br-bright."

Rowdy, now feeling a little bolder, walked up to Boo. Trying to look him in both crossed eyes at the same time, he said, "Who's not bright, you goofy looking bird? I've got a good mind to knock your eyes uncrossed for you, Mr. Boo or Boo-Boo or whatever your silly name is!"

Sassy quickly moved to Rowdy's side and said, "Please forgive my brother. He's just a little upset at our strange experience. Will you please tell us who is this Wizard you speak of?"

"Yes," asked Kevin, "what kind of strange place are we in and how come I can understand what the animals are saying?"

"Questions, questions," said Boo, who hopped close to Rowdy's face. "You are in a pl-place like no other place y-you have ever b-been b-before. Th-the Wizard will answer all your questions and the only thing strange h-here is this little brown ball of talking fur and-and it's pointed little n-nose!" At that Boo flew into the air and said, "Follow me down the corridor and the Wizard will see y-you."

24

Rowdy, angered further at Boo's last stab at him, reached into his back pocket, pulled out his slingshot, placed a small pebble on it, and drew aim on Boo. He murmured, "Take this, you oversized, flying, cross-eyed moth."

But Kevin quickly jerked the slingshot from Rowdy. "No, little fellow, that's not the right way. Come, both of you, climb up on my shoulders and let's go see this Wizard."

With Sassy and Rowdy riding on his shoulders, Kevin followed Boo down the corridor, through the Outer Chamber to the doors of the Inner Chamber. Boo instructed them to wait: Willard would open the doors to the Inner Chamber when he was ready to see them. Flying away, he could not resist one last taunt at Rowdy, who was still sitting on Kevin's shoulder. As he flew by, he thumped Rowdy on the ear with the tip of his wing and chuckled a little.

The outraged Rowdy shook his fist at Boo flying away and called after him, "When I get you out of here, I'm gonna stuff you in a gopher hole!"

Back at the old farm, the storm was over. Uncle Jim called in help from the small town to search for Kevin. Charles, Samantha, Tommy, and Donna were already in the forest looking for him.

In the forest, all the animals gathered to look for Sassy and Rowdy.

Chapter 4

Willard the Wizard

Kevin, Sassy, and Rowdy sat outside the door of the Inner Chamber and waited for Willard to admit them.

Inside the Inner Chamber, Willard gazed into the Oracle, seeking instructions from the Sagittarians. Using the power of the Oracle, he showed King Benjamin, the ruler of the Sagittarians, all the images and events that had transpired. King Benjamin instructed Willard how to proceed.

The door to the Inner Chamber slowly opened. Sassy and Rowdy quickly climbed atop of the boy's shoulders again as Kevin cautiously entered the Inner Chamber. Standing before them was Willard, holding a staff in his right hand. He was clothed in a purple robe, and hanging from a long, gold chain about his neck was a brilliant medallion that glowed emerald.

Kevin spoke very carefully. "Are you the Wizard, sir?"

"Yes," replied Willard, "and you are Kevin and your two young friends are Sassy and Rowdy Krackers. Kevin, you live with your Uncle Jim, one brother, Tommy, and one sister, Donna. Sassy, you and Rowdy live in the old hickory with your father, Sebastian."

The little visitors were simply amazed that he knew all this. Sassy then asked, "Did you save us from the Giant Wa-

terfalls?"

"Yes," answered Willard.

"Well, we thank you very much," replied Sassy.

"Where are we?" asked Kevin.

"You are in the land of the Enchanted Valley," said Willard.

Rowdy now joined the conversation. "Why did you bring us here . . . and who is that dumb bat outside?"

Willard chuckled. "That is Boo. I watched the two of you taunting each other. My little friend, do not judge Boo too harshly. He can and will become a very loyal and good friend to you."

Kevin said, "I have several questions, sir. Why did you save us? Why did you bring us here? How do you know so much about us? How can I be talking to and understanding the animals?"

Willard looked at the three for a moment then replied, "I am not permitted to answer all your questions in detail at this time. However, I will answer as much as I am permitted. I saved you from the Giant Waterfalls because your hearts are noble. I brought you here so I could talk with you and test the Light of Goodness that dwells in your hearts. What I know about you and your families I was told by King Benjamin. And to your final question, you are inside a power source of knowledge and so long as you remain inside these walls you will be able to understand each other."

Sassy asked, "Who is King Benjamin?"

Willard walked over to the Oracle, which was now glowing yellow. His eyes pierced deep into it, while he received further instructions to his mind from King Benjamin. After a few moments of silence, he looked at them and said, "My precious friends, before I answer any more of your questions, please allow me to ask a favor of you."

Kevin replied, "We owe you our lives. Please ask us what you wish."

"Well," said Willard, "please approach the Oracle and place your hands upon it. I promise it will not harm you."

Rowdy, remembering the many pranks he had played on others, suspiciously asked, "Oh, yeah? Whatcha want us to do that for?"

Willard, understanding Rowdy's thoughts, once again chuckled and said, "My little prankster friend, the Oracle will simply measure the Light of Goodness that dwells in you."

They agreed and approached to place their hands upon the Oracle. The Oracle lit up brightly and began to change from one brilliant color to another, until it ran through all the colors in the rainbow.

"Wonderful!" replied Willard. "This is even greater than I had expected. Now come and sit, my friends. Our time together grows short. I must soon send you back to your families, because they are worried and are searching for you."

As the three sat in a semicircle around Willard on the floor, Rowdy asked, "How do you know our families are searching for us?"

Willard replied, "King Benjamin has told me."

"Who is King Benjamin?" asked Sassy again.

Willard looked lovingly at the three and responded, "Please do not ask any more questions at this time. Allow me

to use our short time to tell you a story. I believe it will answer as many of your questions as I am permitted to let you know at this time."

The little group listened intently as Willard began. "A few thousand years ago there was a race of highly advanced people that dwelled on a planet far, far from here. They were a happy people living at peace with each other and all things around them. The sun that warmed their world was about to explode, so they searched the heavens and found that this planet was suitable to support their life. So they came here. But upon arriving, they found that this planet was already occupied by the human and animal families.

"Now, my little friends, you must understand, the Sagittarians had great knowledge and power and could have easily taken your world from you. But because of the Light of Goodness within them they could not use their knowledge or power to take away a world that belonged to someone else. They sat in council with each other and resolved that they would live on this planet and not interfere with the existing population, except in matters of goodness, such as your rescue."

Willard stopped his story for a moment and, looking at Rowdy, said, "King Benjamin has taken a liking to you, because he, like you, Rowdy, is good, but he has a mischievous spirit about him. The Sagittarians are very small, about six inches in height. They are loving people. The Light of Goodness burns brightly in them. This colony has lived in the Enchanted Valley in seclusion from the ever-expanding human population. King Benjamin and his Council have observed all that has transpired today and are watching us now through the power of the Oracle. The Oracle is one of the many advanced instruments they brought with them when they came to this world."

Rowdy, who was totally fascinated by this, got up and walked over to the Oracle. He peered into it and said, "I don't see the little dwarfs."

Willard shook his head and said, "Rowdy, they are not hiding in the Oracle and you should be careful about calling King Benjamin a dwarf. Remember, Rowdy, King Benjamin is good, but like you, he knows many pranks, and I wouldn't provoke that side of his nature."

"Oh," said Rowdy, "please tell His Tininess that I meant no disrespect."

"You may tell him yourself, because here he comes."

Suddenly, the Oracle turned brilliant green and out popped King Benjamin, all decked out in a bright orange robe with a teeny little gold crown on his head. His tiny nose twitched and his little white beard pointed straight out. He leaped directly in front of the young raccoon. Rowdy backed up with his fur standing up on end. His eyes widened in astonishment at the sight of the little king, now standing directly in front of him.

"His Tininess!" exclaimed King Benjamin. "Dwarfs, you say!"

Rowdy, gulping to swallow, declared, "I thought you said he wasn't in there!"

"Well," said King Benjamin, "I wasn't in there, my little mischievous friend. I just used its power to transport myself here so I could be getting a closer look at the likes of you." He continued, "You know, Willard, I could turn him into a horse

31

and ride him across the valley. Or, better than that, I'll make him a mouse and let the cats chase him."

Sassy quickly approached King Benjamin and spoke up for Rowdy, who for once was so terrified he was unable to speak. "Please, good king, do not hurt him. He meant no harm."

King Benjamin reared back, holding his pudgy belly, and laughingly replied, "My sweet, darling Sassy, I'm not going to harm him. But would you look at that pitiful, frightened expression on his face!" And once again King Benjamin burst into laughter. Rowdy said nothing, realizing he had met his match in the little king.

King Benjamin then turned to Willard and stated, "Their families are extremely worried. It is time to send them back." Looking now at Rowdy, he said, "Rowdy, my friend, you are a critter after my own heart. I shall see you again on another day." With that he took one leap and disappeared back through the Oracle, which then returned to its yellow color.

"My goodness," said Kevin, "things sure come and go in a strange way around here!"

Rowdy wiped his forehead with the back of his paw and said, with a sigh of relief, "Wow, that was a close one!"

Willard now pulled a ring from his finger and said, "Kevin, give me your hand, please." Kevin did as he was instructed. Willard placed the ring on the boy's finger and said, "My boy, King Benjamin has instructed me to give you this ring. It will connect you to the power of the Oracle. Now, Kevin, listen very carefully to what I am about to tell you. Because the Light of Goodness is so strong in you and your brother and sister, and for other reasons which we shall not totally reveal at this time, the Sagittarians have chosen you to help them avoid the possibility of a future threat to them and the animal kingdom of the Big Thicket. If this possible threat to their safety becomes a reality, then the Sagittarians will be forced to make a very difficult decision."

"What decision?" asked Kevin.

Willard's face hardened in deep concern as he replied, "In order for the Sagittarians to survive they will have to re-

32

locate or openly confront the human population." Willard paused for a second, then, placing both hands on the lad's shoulders and looking him directly in the eye, said, "Now, Kevin, I want you to clearly understand that should these things happen it will not mean that you or your family would have to come to the aid of the Sagittarians or the animal kingdom. It only means there is a way you could assist if you wish to."

Kevin was uncertain of exactly what threat Willard referred to, but quickly answered, "I don't know how I could possibly help, but you can count on me and I'm certain you can depend upon my family to assist you."

"Yes," replied Willard, "I can see that in your eyes. Now let me tell you about the ring. Lad, because the ring is connected to the Oracle, it has many uses and an awesome power. However, I am only going to instruct you in two of its lesser abilities."

Pointing with his finger to the center of the ring, Willard continued, "Do you see the large A?" Kevin nodded his head. "If you turn the letter A one-quarter turn to the right, it will allow you to understand what the animals are saying to you once you are outside this room. If you turn it straight upside down and concentrate on me or King Benjamin, it will project an image of us before you which will enable you to talk with us. Also, if the ring starts glowing, you will know we are about to contact you. Your brother's and sister's thought patterns have also been programmed into the ring. This means the ring will work for any one of you or all three of you together. The ring will not work for any other human, and only the three of you will be able to understand the animals or see our projected images when the ring is being used.

"Now, Kevin, let me warn you. This is not a toy. Use it only when necessary. Do not play with it or experiment with it for other use except what I have told you. If it becomes necessary to use it for greater things, I will instruct you in its use at that time. Now it is time for you to leave. I have told you all I'm permitted to for now. It would be best if you spoke to no other humans except your brother and sister about this."

"Willard," asked Kevin, "may I ask two more questions

33

before we go?"

"Yes, but make them quick."

Looking at his new friend and feeling a strange sense of devotion toward him, Kevin asked, "Are you and Boo of this world or did you come here with the Sagittarians?"

Willard answered, "Boo is of this world. He was in an accident one night in another storm. His guidance system that enables bats to see was destroyed. The Sagittarians found him, and King Benjamin had them install some mechanical eyes. However, King Benjamin, having a sense of humor, had them installed crossed. Now, do not misunderstand, they work just fine. As for myself, I am of neither world. In your terms of understanding, I am an android robot, built by the Sagittarians to watch over the Oracle. I think and function and feel emotions of good. Now go, my friends, to the old door and sit upon it and I will send you back to your point of origin."

The little group left their friend and went back down the corridor to the hidden entrance of the magnesium tree. There Boo opened the entrance and they said goodbye to him as they went out. Rowdy was last to pass by Boo and was trying to think of something to say when Boo said, "See you around the gopher holes, Fuzzy Wuzzy!" Rowdy looked back over his shoulder, smiled his mischievous little grin, and thought, *There will be another day.* He climbed aboard the old door.

Willard placed his hands upon the Oracle and concentrated on the images of his friends outside. The old door rose into the air with the little travelers cuddling together. Then it sailed across the countryside with great speed until it arrived at the point on the creek where the old shack had stood. There it gently lowered to the ground.

In the distance, Kevin could hear Uncle Jim, Tommy, and Donna calling for him. Looking at Sassy and Rowdy, he said, "I'm going to miss you." He waited for them to reply, then realized they were no longer in the place of knowledge. He couldn't understand what they were trying to say to him.

Sassy reached out, lifted his hand, and pointed to the ring. "Oh, yes," responded Kevin as he turned the A one-quarter turn to the right.

34

Then he heard Sassy say, "We're going to miss you too, Kevin, but if you come to the forest we can have great adventures together and we will introduce you to all our friends."

Kevin told them he would return as soon as possible and, getting on his knees, he leaned over and hugged both of his precious new friends. With a tear in his eye, he said, "Goodbye."

As darkness closed over the forest, Kevin walked toward the sound of his family calling for him. He glanced over his shoulder to see Sassy and Rowdy, still standing on the old door, waving goodbye.

Chapter 5

Tommy Finds Rowdy

Night had settled over the forest. Sassy and Rowdy had a joyous reunion with their father and friends, who had been searching for them. As Sebastian tucked them into bed, they related the entire events of the day to him.

Sebastian listened with interest as they told him about Willard and the threat to the animals of the Big Thicket.

"What kind of threat?" asked Sebastian.

Sassy answered, "I don't know, Papa, but it must be awfully serious."

Rowdy chimed in, "Yeah, and Kevin can understand us and he will bring the other two children to the forest and we can get to know them and, Papa, they can learn from us." He paused for a second and wiggled down in his covers, then sighed, "I'll betcha they know all kinds of super pranks they can teach me." With this wonderful thought on his mind, he slipped quietly into sleep.

Sebastian kissed both good night and walked over to the round window in the old hickory. He looked back at them as they lay sleeping in their beds. He gazed at the stars, thinking about their mother. A tear trickled down and dropped off the end of his nose as he sighed and whispered, "Oh, Amanda,

my sweet, darling Amanda, how much they need you and how much I miss you."

As the moon rose over the old farm, Kevin gathered Tommy and Donna into his room to tell them about the ring and Willard. Both children sat astonished at the story.

Tommy said, "Let's get Pete's big old fat cat, Pussywillow, in here and try the ring on him."

Kevin reminded them about Willard's warning not to use the ring idly, "But I guess it's okay, because I have to show you how it works."

Tommy found the cat lying in the kitchen, as that was his favorite place, next to the food. He quickly returned to the room lugging the large orange and black cat by the shoulders. Now, Pussywillow doesn't take kindly to being awakened and dragged off to the children's room. When Kevin turned the ring on and Pussywillow found himself carrying on a two-sided conversation with humans, he decided it was either a nightmare or his mind had absorbed too much catnip. Whatever the explanation, he wanted nothing to do with it. He leaped through the open window into a treetop, then, bounding to the ground, he went squalling into the night.

The children decided that upon arising in the morning they would go into the forest and find Sassy and Rowdy and meet all of their friends. The three children then retired to bed.

After the extraordinary day Kevin had been through, sleep came upon him quickly. And so it was with Donna. Tommy, on the other hand, lay in bed only napping. Tossing and turning, he was restless and impatient. Glorious thoughts danced about in his mind and robbed him of his sleep. He imagined the exciting adventures he would have talking and sharing experiences with all the animals of the forest and the wonder of meeting Willard and King Benjamin and on and on until at last sleep was hopeless. Kevin, he thought to himself, had had a hard day and would probably want to sleep until at least noon. Donna had just worn herself out worrying. *Well, now*, thought Tommy, *I can't wait until noon, so I will just get up at sunrise and go into the forest with the ring and spend a couple of hours before Kevin and Donna awaken. After all, it would not be very thoughtful of me to expect them to get up that early when they have had such a difficult day.*

So, at the first crack of dawn, Tommy was up and dressed. He slipped the ring from Kevin's finger. Quickly, he was out the door and down the hill into the forest.

After venturing a reasonable distance into the forest, he decided it was time to give the ring a whirl. He turned the big A a quarter turn to the right and began to scout around for the first animals. As his eyes scanned about, he noticed a large mound of dirt with a hole right in the center of it. "Well," said Tommy, "let's see if anybody's home." He leaned over the hole and, pounding on top of it, yelled down, "Anybody home?"

"Home, home," came the reply from down below, "who in tarnation wants to know if anybody's home, anyway? A body can't get any peace and quiet for all the racket you're making up there!" Up popped a funny little head with two little black eyes and two big buck teeth. Snorting and blowing, he continued, "Who's a bangin' on my house anyway? I-I'm —" Then, seeing the human child, he quickly ducked back in.

Tommy banged and yelled loudly down the hole again,

"Come on out, Mr. Gopher. I want to talk to you." He waited
a moment and when there was no reply he started to shout
louder down the hole, "I won't hurt you, I just want to talk to
you."

Before Tommy could move his face away from the hole,
out came the little gopher's head. With their faces just inches
apart, the gopher yelled back, "Hey, boy, you think I'm deaf?
Well, I'm going to be if you don't stop that infernal yelling."
The gopher climbed out and sat on the mound, shaking the
fallen dirt off his fur, and asked, "All right, boy, now that
you've made a nuisance out of yourself and almost caved my
roof in on me, what in the infernal tarnation do you want?"

"Well," the boy said, "my name's Tommy and I live on
the old farm at the edge of the forest. What do folks call you?"

Quite annoyed, the gopher replied, "Human folks call me
a pest, but that's what they ought to be calling you. To the critters of the forest I am known as Gabby. The hole is my home —
or it was until you darn near beat it down on top of me."

"Oh, I'm sorry, Gabby," said Tommy.

"Well, that's good to know," said Gabby, "but you sure couldn't prove it by me. Now, boy, tell me before I go back down and try to repair what is left of my house, is there anything else I can do for you?"

"Yes," replied Tommy, "please tell me where I can find Rowdy and Sassy Krackers."

Gabby hopped around the mound and asked, "Do you know Sassy and Rowdy?"

"Well, I don't know them, but my brother does and I want to meet them."

Gabby's eyes bugged out and his nose twitched as he asked, "You got a brother?"

"Yes," said Tommy, "and a sister too."

"Well," asked Gabby, "are they comin' this way too, and do they go around trying to beat a body's house down on top of him? 'Cause if they do, then I'd best be getting to work on it or I'll have nothing left but a heap of dirt!"

"No," said Tommy, "they won't beat your house down on you. They are very kind."

"Well," snorted Gabby, "it's good for a body to know that destructiveness doesn't run in your family. Let's see," he continued, "what was it you wanted to know now?"

Tommy repeated that he would like to know where Sassy and Rowdy lived.

"Oh, yes, I remember now," replied Gabby, "it's no wonder I forgot. You almost gave me a concussion, beating on the top of my house. Well, anyway, go straight ahead to the big elm and turn left."

"What big elm?" interrupted Tommy.

"Are you blind, boy, or are you just stupid? It's right in front of you! Well, anyhow, if you have enough sense to find the big elm, you turn left and go straight until you come to the large old hickory. That's where they live. Oh, and by the way, boy, when you get there, try not to knock their walls down on top of them." With that Gabby disappeared back into his hole, muttering and tossing dirt out of the top of it.

Tommy went straight to the big elm, turned left, and walked until he saw a large old hickory. As he approached he saw a small brown raccoon climbing out of one of the holes.

Tommy shouted up, "Are you Rowdy?"

The little raccoon replied, "Yes, I'm Rowdy, who are you?"

"I'm Tommy."

Upon hearing that, Rowdy bounded down the old hickory to a limb that was at head level with Tommy and said, "I see you got the ring on. Where's my friend Kevin?"

"He's home asleep," answered Tommy, "and probably will not awaken until noon. I just wanted to meet you and Sassy and some of your friends. Will the two of you show me around the forest?"

"Well," said Rowdy, "Sassy's sleeping late, too, but I will be glad to show you around if you like."

"That's great. Jump on my shoulder and let's go!"

Rowdy leaped onto Tommy's shoulder. He held on to Tommy's ear with one paw, pointed with the other, and ordered, "Thataway, boy!"

The two strolled through the forest for a short time. Suddenly, Tommy said, "My goodness, what is that I smell?"

Rowdy explained, "We are downwind of old Lonesome."

"Who is Lonesome?" Tommy asked.

"You'll see in a moment. We are about to pass by his den. Sassy says we must always be polite to Lonesome and pretend we don't smell anything. But I'll tell you something, Tommy, you be sure when we get there that you get upwind of him before we start talking to him. It is sure a heck of a lot easier to pretend when you are upwind!"

As the two rounded the bend in the path, they saw Lonesome Skunk out in front of his den, scratching in the leaves for bugs. "Whatcha doin', Lonesome?" asked Rowdy.

"Oh, I'm just getting a little air," answered Lonesome as he turned around to face them. When Lonesome saw Tommy he became frightened and whirled about, throwing his tail up in the air and taking aim.

Rowdy shouted, "Don't you dare spray him! I'm riding on his shoulders. I swear, Lonesome, if you spray that junk on me, I'll knock your stripes into polka dots!"

"Oh," Lonesome said as he lowered his aim and turned back to face them. "He's a human . . . aren't you afraid of him?"

Rowdy peeked out from behind Tommy's head, where he had taken shelter to avoid being hit by Lonesome's shot. "This is one of the human children that Charles belongs to."

"Oh," said Lonesome, "well, how do you do?"

Tommy, who had temporarily frozen in his tracks, replied, "Well, when my legs stop shaking, I think I will do fine."

The three had a good laugh together before Lonesome announced, "Sassy and Rowdy have told all the animals of the forest about you and your family. All through last night the critters spread the word about the ring and how they could talk to you."

"Well," said Rowdy, "we've got to be on our way."

"Where you going?" asked Lonesome.

Rowdy replied, "I think we're going to go down to Fangs' cave and see if old Fangs is around."

The two told Lonesome goodbye and headed toward Fangs' cave.

Chapter 6

Old Fangs

"Who is old Fangs?" asked Tommy as they walked toward the cave.

"He's a very big and very old snake," replied Rowdy.

"Will he bite us?"

"Well, he might, if he had any fangs. A couple of years ago Hunter John ran over his head with the jeep and broke out his fangs. Ever since then, he hasn't been right in the head and the only thing he can bite is his own nose."

The two arrived at the cave and found old Fangs hanging from the limb of a wild plum tree, sniffing and sucking on the blossoms.

"Hi there, old Fangs," said Rowdy.

Old Fangs raised his head and, with his bottom lip bumping his nose, replied, "Hi ya there, Rowdy. Is this one of your human friends all the critters are talking about?"

Rowdy answered, "Yes, this is Tommy."

Old Fangs curled up and raised his head back as if he was going to strike and, with as mean a look as he could get on his toothless face, sneered, "Do I frighten you, boy?"

Tommy, looking old Fangs in the face, began to giggle at the sight of the snake's wrinkled lips curling around his empty mouth. "No," said Tommy, "I think you're cute!"

"Oh, gosh," whined old Fangs, "you sure know how to hurt a fella!"

Tommy was bewildered by Fangs' statement. "Why?"

"Well," said Fangs, "I'm a snake. I am supposed to strike fear in the hearts of everybody, but the only fear I can strike in anybody is that they might die laughing by just looking at me."

"There, there," said Tommy, "I didn't mean to hurt your feelings. My grandpa didn't have any teeth and I loved him."

"You did?" asked Fangs. "Why?"

"Well," replied Tommy, "because he spent his life doing good for others and was worthy of everybody's love."

"Oh, I don't know about doing good," said old Fangs. "Is it painful?"

"No, it will make you happy."

Old Fangs slithered down the limb a piece and asked, "Did everybody laugh at him because he looked funny in the face?"

No, because he had false teeth that he wore in his mouth," Tommy answered.

"Oh," sighed Fangs, "I would give anything for some false fangs, just so I wouldn't look so funny and nobody would laugh at me."

Tommy walked around the limb, looking at old Fangs, while he conjured up an idea. "Tell me," said Tommy, "if you had some false fangs, would you use them to hurt anybody?"

"Oh, no," declared Fangs, "I promise I wouldn't hurt a soul."

"Well," said Tommy, "I can make you some false fangs."

"You can?" cried Fangs. He got so excited he lost his grip on the limb and fell to the ground on his back. Flipping this way and that way, he managed to turn himself right side up. Raising his head as high as he could, with his lips flapping together in great excitement, he begged, "Will you, oh, will you please?"

Tommy pulled his pocket knife from his hip pocket and said, "My grandpa taught me how to carve and whittle, so I'm going to make you some false fangs out of wood. But remember, you promised not to hurt anyone with them."

"Oh, I promise, I promise, I PROMISE!" swore Fangs.

Tommy set Rowdy down and found a large piece of white pine, then began carving on it. "Come," he said, "get right in front of me and hold your mouth open so I can measure it." Old Fangs sat patiently in front of the boy with his mouth open while Tommy worked on the wood carving. Then Tommy put the wood carving in Fang's mouth, marked it, and carved some more. Finally, he said, "Now it's all done." He placed the wooden set of fangs in the snake's mouth and asked, "How do they fit?"

Old Fangs cocked his head back with a new sense of self-respect and pride. "They fit great, and it feels so good not to slap the end of my nose with my bottom lip when I talk." Fangs slinked over to a pool of water and looked into it, admiring his reflection. He grinned and flashed his new choppers. Tilting his head from side to side, he said, "Ain't they just beautiful!" Wriggling back over to Tommy, he said, "I thank you very much. And now I must go and try them out."

45

"Remember," reminded Tommy, "you promised not to hurt anything."

"Oh, the field mice that live over by the meadow have been taunting me for a long time because they know I can't bite them. I'm going to slip over there and put a little respect back into them, but I promise I won't hurt them."

Rowdy declared, "You mean, you're going to flash your fangs and scare the living daylights out of them."

"Yeah, yeah," admitted Fangs. He nodded his head with a huge grin and a hiss. "Oh," he said, "I haven't been able to hiss for two years and it feels so good." Old Fangs thanked Tommy again and slithered away toward the meadow.

Chapter 7

Great Jumpin' Jehoshaphats

It was approaching midmorning as Tommy and Rowdy sat at the edge of the pool by old Fangs' cave. Tommy turned to Rowdy and said, "You were there when Willard gave Kevin the ring."

"Yeah," replied Rowdy.

"Well," mused Tommy, "I wonder what would happen if we turned the A all the way around?"

A mischievous grin came over Rowdy's face. "I don't know," he said. "Willard said it had a lot of magic in it."

"Magic?" asked Tommy.

"Well, he didn't say magic, but that's what I'm sure he meant. Why don't we try and see what happens?"

Both having curious and mischievous natures, they couldn't stand the mystery of it any longer. Rowdy climbed up into Tommy's lap, reached down, and turned the big A the rest of the way around. The ring began to hum and vibrate, shaking the ground around them. Little streams of colored lights shot out as Tommy exclaimed, "Great Jumpin' Jehoshaphats!"

He tried to hold his hand steady, then suddenly everything was quiet and a peculiar voice said, "Here I am."

Rowdy leaped upon Tommy's shoulder and cried, "Who said that?"

The voice replied, "Why, I did, of course."

"Who are you?" asked Tommy.

"Well," the voice answered, "I guess I am the Great Jumpin' Jehoshaphats."

"I don't see you," said Rowdy, "where are you?"

"You don't see me," responded the voice, "because you haven't imagined what I look like in your minds."

With that statement both Tommy and Rowdy imagined what the voice would look like. When this happened the little colored lights shot up from the ring, bounced off their heads, and came to a point together in front of them. Then, in a glorious burst of brilliant fireworks, there he stood before them. He was purple and orange and green. He had the legs of a kangaroo, the body of a fat horse, the neck and head of a dragon, and two small wings just behind his front shoulders.

"Oh, my gosh," said Tommy.

"No," replied the Jumpin' Jehoshaphats, "I can't be your gosh. I do not believe I am a gosh. I am whatever the both of you imagine me to be."

"That's not what I meant," said Tommy. "That's only an expression."

"Well," said the Jumpin' Jehoshaphats, "I came into being because, while you had the ring turned on imaginary images, you used another expression and created me."

Rowdy jumped to Tommy's lap and shouted, "Turn it off, turn it off quick, before we create no tellin' what!" Tommy quickly turned the big A back to where it had been. Rowdy jumped back on Tommy's shoulder and said, "Why are you still here? You'd better disappear before we get into all kinds of trouble!"

"I don't know if I can disappear," admitted the creature. "I don't know anything about what I can do."

Rowdy leaped to the ground and, placing his hands on his hips, said, "Besides being big and ugly, you're pretty stupid too."

"If I am stupid, it's because you're stupid. I came from your minds."

This angered the little raccoon and he walked up in front of the Jumpin' Jehoshaphats. "Well, you look like a dragon in the face. Can you breathe fire?"

"I don't know," said the Jumpin' Jehoshaphats, "but I'll try." He opened his mouth and blew forth a stream of fire that almost roasted Rowdy, who was still standing in front of him.

Rowdy, jumping around, slapping at his smoking, singed fur, cried, "You fool, watch where you're breathing! You darn near cooked me."

Tommy sat staring at the Jumpin' Jehoshaphats, still astonished at his appearance, then asked, "What are we going to do with you?"

"What do you want to do with me?" asked the creature.

"I know what I'm going to do with you if you ever breathe on me again," growled Rowdy, still angry as smoke drifted about his ears.

"Well," asked Tommy, "what shall we call you?"

"Whatever pleases you," he answered.

"I think Jumpin' Jehoshaphats is too long a name. How about just calling you Gee?" suggested Tommy.

"If it pleases you," replied Gee.

Gee waited silently while Tommy and Rowdy huddled to discuss what to do with him. The two approached Gee, and Tommy asked, "Can you go back to where you came from?"

"I don't know how."

"Well," said Rowdy, "if you can't go back and we're stuck with you, let's see what you can do." Rowdy, looking Gee over and carefully remembering the results of the last thing he asked Gee to do, said, "Without landing on top of me and squashing me like a bug, let's see how high you can jump with those enormous hind legs of yours."

"Okay," said Gee, "I'll try." He leaped into the air, rising as high as the trees. Then, fluttering his small wings, he returned to the ground.

"Wow! Superfantastic!" exclaimed Rowdy. "Now be still a minute, dumbo, while I get on top of you and let's do that again." Rowdy scurried up Gee's tail all the way to his neck and got a firm grip. "All right, now, you oversized grasshopper. Do it again."

Gee leaped into the air again. Rowdy let out a wild

50

screech of sheer delight as they fluttered back to the ground. His eyes sparkled with delight as he exclaimed, "What a ride!" He looked at Tommy and said, "Come on and get up here with me." Tommy climbed up on Gee beside Rowdy, who leaned over and patted Gee on the side of his neck and confided, "Old boy, I think I'm gonna like havin' you around! Now, old Gee, I want to see how far up and how far out you can jump."

Now, in all the days of the Big Thicket, there had never been such a strange sight to behold. Gee leaped into the air and covered great distances, fluttered back to the ground, then leaped again. Through the forest they traveled on top of the strange creature, a small boy and a raccoon, laughing and squealing in pure ecstasy.

At last they had Gee stop for a rest and Tommy said, "It's getting late in the morning and I have to go home before Kevin gets up. What are we going to do with Gee?"

Rowdy replied, "Well, first, I will give you a lift to the edge of the forest. Then I'm going to ride my old pal about the forest and hope I see Hunter John's dogs, Spike and Otis. If I do, I'm going to have old Gee breathe a little life into them, if you get my meaning."

"Okay," said Tommy, "but then you should take him to Fangs' cave and tell him to hide there until we can decide what to do with him." The two agreed, and Tommy and Rowdy rode Gee to the edge of the forest. There Tommy started walking toward home.

Rowdy, who had climbed up on top of Gee's head and was holding on to his ears like horse reins, rode into the forest to hide old Gee in Fangs' cave.

Chapter 8

What To Do With Gee

After some time spent leaping through the forest on Gee and terrorizing the critters, Rowdy returned to old Fangs' cave and instructed Gee to remain in hiding there. Then he returned to the old hickory and related to Sassy all the wonderful events.

Tommy had returned to the old farm, where he found Kevin and Donna furiously waiting for him. After receiving a severe scolding from them, he proceeded to tell them about Gee. The three children decided that they must go to old Fangs' cave and use the ring to project Willard's image before them. They would show him Gee and ask his advice about what to do.

Having some chores to do first, the children sent Charles and Samantha ahead to tell Sassy and Rowdy to meet them at old Fangs' cave. Upon completing their chores, the children left the old farm and hurried through the forest.

Suddenly, they saw Gee coming straight at them. Atop of his head, holding on to Gee's ear with one paw and waving with the other, was Rowdy. Sassy was astraddle Gee's neck, holding tightly to his wings. Charles sat proudly upon Gee's back, holding on to one of Gee's wings with his teeth, and Sa-

mantha was riding on Gee's tail. She was whining, "Oh, dear me, I'd much rather walk!"

When they reached the children, Rowdy pulled back on Gee's ears and shouted, "Whoa!" Gee responded instantly to the command and they came to a sudden halt. Rowdy went flying off Gee's head, tumbled end over end through the air, and landed in a briar bush. "Ouch, ouch!" yelled Rowdy as he scrambled out of the briars and headed straight for Gee with an annoyed look on his face.

Gee lowered his head to the ground. His bottom lip drooped and, remorsefully, he said, "I know, you don't have to fuss at me. I stopped too quick again."

The annoyed Rowdy walked up and, placing his little black nose against Gee's nose, said, "Once today you left me hanging in the treetop 'cause you didn't duck your head, and this is the second time you have thrown me through the air. Now, what have I told you?"

His eyes drooping in disappointment, Gee replied, "You told me to always duck my head when I go under limbs and when I stop, to stop slowly."

"Well," said Rowdy, "before you injure me further, will you please try and remember that?"

Raising his head and smiling, Gee said, "Yes, I will . . . yes, I will."

Pulling a briar sticker from his fur, Rowdy spoke to the children. "Hop on and we'll ride him back to the cave."

Kevin and Donna, admiring Gee, climbed on behind Tommy, and away they all rode. Leaping through the air, they were all laughing and enjoying the thrill — except for Samantha, who was still nervously hanging on to the tail.

As they approached old Fangs' cave, Rowdy, wanting to show off, stood on top of Gee's head and shouted, "Look, no hands!" Gee took the final leap that would place them at the cave. Rowdy, still standing on Gee's head, looking back at his friends, realized Gee was about to stop and cried out, "Oh, no!" He desperately grabbed for one of Gee's ears, but it was too late. Once again, the little raccoon flew through the air end over end, landing with a splash in the pool outside Fangs' cave.

As the little raccoon came stomping out of the water, he passed old Fangs, who was lying on a large rock in the sun. Fangs raised his head and said to Rowdy, "Strange time of day to be taking a bath."

Snorting water from his nose, Rowdy snapped, "Just shut up, you wooden-toothed, oversized worm!"

With his temper hot, he headed toward Gee, but Sassy stopped him and said, "Now, mind your temper, Rowdy. It was your own fault. You were showing off." Taking a moment to think about it, Rowdy shook the water from his fur and sat down on a log to dry in the sun.

"Well," said Kevin, "it is time to face the music for what we have done. I'm going to project Willard's image here, tell him that we have misused the ring, and see what we should do." Turning the big A straight down, he concentrated on Willard. In a few seconds, standing before them was Willard's sparkling image.

Before Kevin could speak, Willard said, "I am very disappointed that you have used the ring in an improper manner."

Tommy stepped forward and said, "Mr. Willard, sir, it

54

was I who experimented with it. Kevin didn't know anything about what was happening. If you are angry, please take it out on me. It was my fault."

Willard replied, "It is not our way to take anything out on anyone." Then Willard looked at all of them standing around Kevin and asked, "Have you learned the dangers of misusing the power of the ring?"

"Yes," they all replied.

"Well, then," said Willard, "we shall not dwell on the subject of why you should not have done it. We'll simply decide how to handle the situation at hand." Willard looked the colorful and curious Gee over and said, "Tommy, what a vivid imagination you and Rowdy have!"

"What can we do about Gee?" asked Kevin.

"You can't do anything about him. He has come into being and now he will be forever." Willard paused for a moment in deep meditation, then went on, "King Benjamin has just informed me that he is leaving his hidden castle to come there and join you."

Rowdy jumped off the log and asked, "Is he going to come poppin' out of a rock or something like that?"

"No," replied Willard, "he is using his air scooter to travel there."

Kevin then asked, "Is he coming to punish us or take away the ring?"

"No," said Willard, "I told you before. The Sagittarians do not punish or harm anything. They will only defend and protect."

Donna, gathering enough courage to address Willard, said, "Good sir, why, then, is he coming?"

Willard gazed fondly at her for a moment then answered, "My child, you are very beautiful and innocent. Do not fear King Benjamin. He will not harm you. Now, to answer your question, I am not sure why he is coming. But knowing the king as I do and understanding the mischievous and fun-loving side of his nature, I simply believe he cannot stand being left out of all the excitement going on there." Then turning his attention back to Kevin, Willard said, "King Benjamin should arrive there shortly. His air scooter travels at great speed. He will instruct you as to what to do with your creation. Now, is there anything else you wish to know at this time?"

"No," replied Kevin.

"Then peace be with you all," intoned Willard as his image faded from their sight.

Charles and Samantha had been sitting and watching Willard's projected image talking with the children. When he faded from sight, they went over and sniffed about the ground where the image had been standing. Out of the corner of his eye, Charles noticed something moving. As he turned to get a better look, he saw old Fangs moving toward them. "Come, Samantha," he said, "let's go investigate this strange looking fellow."

Just as they got within a few feet of the snake, old Fangs raised his head and flashed his beautiful fangs. Hissing loudly, he lunged at Samantha. The terrified Samantha turned a flip backwards and ran yelping to hide behind Gee.

Old Fangs just flipped over on his back and, kicking his tail and laughing, said, "Oh, that felt so good to be able to frighten something again!"

Tommy called Charles and Samantha to his side and told them, "The old snake won't hurt you. He's just regaining his confidence."

The children gathered around, petting Gee, as they awaited the arrival of King Benjamin.

Chapter 9

The Commitment

At midday a gentle breeze drifted across the forest. In the distance the waiting group heard a high-pitched whistling sound. Looking in the direction of the sound, they could see an object approaching at tremendous speed, traveling about three feet off the ground. The grass was blown flat and the bushes swayed at its passing. A pudgy little man was sitting atop what appeared to be a motorcycle without any wheels. It was held off the ground by air thrusting down and propelled forward by air thrusting out the rear. Circling the small group a couple of times, the king brought his scooter to rest gently on the ground, directly in front of the little group.

"Wow! Neat! Super neat!" exclaimed Rowdy as he rushed over to admire the machine. He thought to himself, *This is just the right size for me . . .*

King Benjamin leaped off his scooter and paced up and down in front of Gee, looking him over from top to bottom. Slapping his hands on his knees, he exclaimed in a tone of admiration, "What a magnificent beast! What all can he do?"

Kevin replied, "We don't know for sure."

"King Benjamin," asked Tommy, "what are we going to do with him? We can't take him home and we can't keep him hidden in the forest forever."

The little king placed his hands on his forehead, thinking for a moment, then answered, "He will have to come to the Enchanted Valley. If discovered here by the human population they would, in ignorance, destroy him or capture and exhibit him as a freak. Neither of these is what you would want. He can come to the Enchanted Valley and we can shrink him to fit our surroundings and make him a citizen of our Enchanted Kingdom."

They were all saddened that they had to give up their friend, but realized it was the only practical thing to do.

"King Benjamin," asked Sassy, "when does he have to leave?"

The little king paced back and forth with his hands clasped behind him, then replied, "I think if you are very careful and keep him hidden from the human population, he can stay here for a few days. But should he be discovered, send him immediately."

King Benjamin noticed that Rowdy was still admiring the air scooter. He walked over to it and said to Rowdy, "Quite a neat machine, don't you think?"

"Yes," said Rowdy, who was now totally overpowered by the splendor of it. The only thought in his mind was how to get the little king to part with it. Rowdy eased over next to King Benjamin and placed his arm around the little king's shoulders. He attempted to butter up the little king by saying, "Benny, old boy, I'll make you a deal."

The little king, realizing he was about to be flim-flammed, said, "Wait a minute, what's this 'Benny, old boy' stuff?"

"Well," responded Rowdy, "we are friends, right?" King Benjamin nodded. Rowdy continued, "Well, you call me by my name, right?" The king nodded once again. "Well, then," said Rowdy, "isn't Benny short for Benjamin?"

"You might say so," answered the king.

"Well, there you have it," stated Rowdy.

"There I have what?" asked the king.

"We are friends. That's why I call you Benny."

"But, Rowdy," said King Benjamin, "in my kingdom, I am the king and I do not have friends."

"You don't? Aren't you awfully lonely?"

"I didn't mean I don't have friends. What I mean is, my friends are also my subjects and they cannot be just my friends."

Rowdy thought for a moment, then said, "Isn't that awfully confusing — to have friends, but because they are also your subjects, they are not your friends, but really they are your friends? And besides that, you're not in your kingdom. You're in my world."

The little king stammered for a minute, trying to sort out what to say, then in frustration said, "Forget it! You may call me Benny while I am in your world, but when you come to mine, it is King Benjamin or Your Majesty. Now, what kind of deal did you have in mind?"

"Well," offered Rowdy, "I will trade you my slingshot, two colored bottles, and six choice striped marbles for your air scooter."

King Benjamin placed both hands on his hips and replied, "Why should I trade you a highly sophisticated machine for that?"

"Well," said Rowdy, "the marbles are true shooters and you would soon win all the marbles in your kingdom."

"But we don't have any marbles in my kingdom," replied King Benjamin.

"All right," said Rowdy, "then you have the best reason of all."

"I'm almost afraid to ask, but what reason?"

"Well, don't you see? It's simple. It would start a whole new thing in your kingdom. You would have a head start on everybody else. Then you would very quickly end up with all of their marbles."

"Bu-but," stammered the little king. "Oh, never mind! I will think about it."

"Okay," said Rowdy, "now can we go for a ride and will you teach me to drive it?"

"Well, since I don't want to get involved in another conversation with you that I would probably lose, go ahead and get on. I will ride behind you and show you how it works."

Rowdy hopped on and King Benjamin climbed on behind him. After giving Rowdy instructions on how to drive it, the pair got under way. The rest of the group stayed behind to play with and take care of Gee.

The wind blew Rowdy's fur flat against him as he zoomed through the forest, dodging trees. The little king kept telling him, "Not so fast, not so fast!"

After cruising about the forest for a while, Rowdy became quite good at operating the scooter. He asked, "Benny, my friend, can we go somewhere special on this?"

"Where did you have in mind?" asked the king.

"Well, I have never seen the children's house, but I know where it is. Can I cruise by there?"

"I guess so," replied King Benjamin, "but then we must return to the others."

"Okay," said Rowdy. Turning the scooter in the direction of the old farm, he was off in a flash. In a matter of minutes they arrived at the old farm.

Pete was on top of the chicken house with a mouth full of nails, repairing the roof. He watched the small scooter approach and circle the barn. Rubbing his eyes he said to himself, "Pete, you have been out in the sun too long."

Rowdy spotted the chickens roaming about the lot and said, "Watch this, Benny." He pointed the little scooter at

60

them and dived through the center of the flock. He laughed in sheer delight as the chickens scattered, leaping and squawking.

The nails began to fall from Pete's mouth as he watched. Rowdy turned and made one final pass through the chickens, then headed toward the forest.

Tossing his hammer in the air, Pete leaped from the roof and ran toward the house shouting, "Jim, Mister Jim, come quickly!"

Uncle Jim met Pete on the porch and asked, "What's wrong, Pete?"

"Oh, I have never seen such a sight! A little raccoon, a tee-ny king on a teeny motorcycle with no wheels, flying thisaway and thataway!"

Pete was so excited and talking so fast that Uncle Jim could barely understand him. Uncle Jim declared, "Whoa, wait a minute, Pete, just slow down and tell me what happened."

Pete took a deep breath, then said, "Mister Jim, I was on the roof of the chicken house, repairing it like you told me to do. A little brown raccoon came riding up on a little motorcycle without wheels that floated through the air very fast. He had a little fat king riding behind him and they was divin' through the chickens and laughin' and they flew away through the forest!"

Uncle Jim stepped forward and looked closely at Pete. "Pete, you must have gotten too hot on that tin roof in our Texas sun. I want you to go sit in the shade for a while and relax."

"But Mister Jim," exclaimed Pete, "I did see it! I think I did, anyway . . ."

Uncle Jim chuckled. "You'll be all right in a little while. Just relax and cool off."

Pete turned and started walking toward the chicken house, saying to himself, "Oh, Pete, you are losin' your mind! Seein' raccoons flyin' and teeny kings. You're in bad shape, old Pete. You'd better take it easy before the little men come and carry you away to the funny farm for sure!"

Zooming back through the forest, Rowdy and King Benjamin soon arrived at Fangs' cave. Sebastian had come to see the strange Gee.

Now word had spread throughout the forest about Gee and the little king. It was decided they would have a gathering in honor of His Royal Highness. Sebastian extended an invitation to King Benjamin to attend the gathering of the animals at Gushing Waterfalls in the afternoon. It was to be in the king's honor and would give all a chance to meet him. King Benjamin graciously accepted. Sebastian left to help make preparations.

King Benjamin spent some time getting to know the children and Sassy and Rowdy. At last it was time to gather at the Gushing Waterfalls. When the king, the children, and the young raccoons arrived they found all the animals of the forest gathered about in groups, awaiting an opportunity to meet King Benjamin.

As the sun sank low in the west, Sassy, Rowdy, and Donna were playing by the waterfalls. King Benjamin and Sebastian were sitting behind them discussing the beauty of the forest. Suddenly, Sassy stopped playing and a tear came to her eye as she said, "Oh, Rowdy, look!" Rowdy joined her and they both sat on a log in front of Sebastian and King Benjamin, staring at the sun's rays as they flickered through the mist of the water and formed a beautiful rainbow. Sassy wondered, "Do you remember what Mama said to us before she was taken away?"

My love is forever
With you in my heart
I'll build you a rainbow
Should we ever be apart

Remember to smile and
Just look — it will be there
Yes, I'll build you a rainbow
So you'll know I'll always care

Rowdy, wiping the tears from his own eyes, answered, "Yeah, Mama said if anything ever happened to her we would always know she was watching over us or thinking about us because she would build us a rainbow. When we saw it we would know she loved us." Rowdy pulled out a small handkerchief his mother had made for him and wiped Sassy's tears from her cheeks. "Please, Sassy, will you sing the song Mama sang to us?"

Sassy cuddled Rowdy close to her, and as they admired the rainbow, she sang their mother's song.

As Sassy finished the last note of the song, she looked at Sebastian, who was wiping the tears from his own eyes. "Papa, do you think Mama is still alive?"

Sebastian sighed, "I don't know. But we must not give up hope. Sassy, Rowdy, I know if she is, her heart is filled with love for us. If she can escape her captors, she will return to us."

King Benjamin was so touched by this scene that his own little beard was sopping wet with tears. He asked Sebastian what had happened to the children's mother. Sebastian related the story about how their mother had been caught in one of Hunter John's traps and carried away before they could set her free.

King Benjamin sat in silence, his little heart breaking, as he watched Sassy and Rowdy, still cuddled together looking at the rainbow. The little king quietly rose and told Sebastian, "I must excuse myself at this time. I have an urgent matter to take care of that requires me to return to my kingdom." Hugging Sassy and Rowdy, he bade all farewell, climbed on his air scooter, and was gone in a flash.

The sun was about to set, so the children said goodbye and started toward home. All the animals began drifting away to their homes, leaving Sebastian, Sassy, and Rowdy gazing at the fading rainbow as the sun set.

Darkness was gathering about him and the wind blew hard against King Benjamin's face as he pushed his air scooter to top speed toward the Enchanted Valley.

Willard was scanning the king's approach on the Oracle, and he could see on the little king's face a look of deep concern and determination. "Boo," Willard said, "open the door in the magnesium tree. King Benjamin is coming here, and I can see that he is deeply troubled about something."

Chapter 10

The Search

Upon his arrival back in the Enchanted Valley, King Benjamin went directly to the magnesium tree and flew his air scooter straight into the Outer Chamber. He instructed Boo to come to the Inner Chamber with him. There Willard greeted him and asked, "What is troubling Your Majesty?"

The little king replied, "We have a job to do. Boo, bring all my captains and advisors to me now." Boo left immediately to carry out the request. "Willard," the king said, "sound the general alarm throughout all the kingdom. Instruct all our people to assemble in the Great Hall so I may speak with them."

"Your Majesty, it is past dark and most are probably fast asleep by now."

"Then wake them," ordered the king as he paced about the Inner Chamber.

"As you wish," replied Willard.

Boo returned shortly with the king's captains and advisors. King Benjamin addressed his advisors first. He told them to prepare maps of all the area from the Red River to the Rio Grande River, including the area known to the human population as Texas.

Then turning to his captains, he said, "Go to the Winged Locust People, to the Flying Horsemen, and to the Woolly Bees and the Lightning Pixies. Have them assemble in the Great Hall at once." All departed from the king's presence to carry out their instructions.

Back in the forest, Sebastian, Rowdy, and Sassy hid Gee in Fangs' cave and returned to their home in the old hickory.

The children and the dogs had returned to the old farm and were gathered about the table for their evening meal. They noticed that Pete was not himself. Donna asked, "What's wrong, Pete? You seem very depressed."

"Missy Donna," replied Pete, "I think I am very ill. I am seein' things that cannot be."

"What kind of things?" asked Tommy.

"You would not believe and would laugh at old Pete."

Kevin said, "We have learned a great many things in the past few days. We won't laugh at you. Please tell us."

Moving a chair very close to the children and turning it backwards, Pete sat down and leaned over, whispering, "Tiny kings, little raccoons riding strange bikes and laughing. That is what I have seen. And now you think old Pete is crazy, right?"

The children smiled at each other and Donna said, "Dear Pete, you are not losing your mind. You have seen what you have seen and we know it is true."

Pete slapped the back of the chair with his hand and said, "How do you know this thing is true? Mister Jim thinks I cooked my brains in the sun. He doesn't believe me."

Kevin replied, "Uncle Jim is as good a man as there is in the world, but he does not understand. There are things in this world that are not of this world."

Looking the children over carefully, Pete said, "You know something special, maybe you tell old Pete, huh?"

"Yes," Tommy said, "we have a very special secret, but we cannot tell you now. Maybe one day we will be able to, but we want you to know that everything is all right and we believe you."

Once again Pete slapped the back of the chair and said, "I will not ask you what your secret is, but I want you to know

that you have made old Pete feel much better. If you ever need old Pete's help . . ." He stopped for a moment and placed his finger over his lips, saying, "Sssh!" Then continuing, ". . . with the tiny king or anything, well, you just let old Pete know."

The hour was growing late. All the critters in the forest were fast asleep and the children prepared for bed. None was aware of the tremendous legion of mercy that was being assembled in the Enchanted Kingdom.

With his hands clasped behind him, King Benjamin paced back and forth in front of Willard. One of the advisors arrived and informed him that all were assembled in the Great Hall awaiting his presence. The king said to Willard, "Come, let us go and speak to our people." Willard and King Benjamin left the Inner Chamber and journeyed down the corridor deep into the hillside until they arrived in the Great Hall.

The king marched to the platform and, looking out at all the inhabitants of the Enchanted Kingdom, spoke, "My friends . . ." He paused a moment, remembering his conversation with Rowdy about friends, then continued, ". . . and I want you to know I have learned new meaning for the word, 'friends.' You are all my subjects, but you are also my precious friends." King Benjamin paused once again to wipe a tear from his eye. "We have an opportunity tonight to enrich and brighten the Light of Good in ourselves. We can add to the wealth of love we feel for each other and for all creatures."

Pointing in the direction of the forest, he continued, "Out there in our forest there are two little hearts yearning for the presence of their mother, who was taken captive by the black-hearted jackal named Hunter John. Somewhere she is being held captive, kept from her family and awaiting certain destruction." The little king stretched both his arms toward his people and asked, "Will you help me find her?"

A roaring cheer came back from all the inhabitants of the Enchanted Kingdom. It was so loud that the walls of the Great Hall shook.

"Yea, yea," they answered, "we will serve our fellow creatures."

King Benjamin was so overwhelmed by the response that he was speechless for a moment. Then he said to them, "Her name is Amanda Krackers. She is a gray raccoon. Each of you has been given a map with an area marked on it. Now go out into the night, my friends, and search all of your area. Ask questions of all forms of life you come in contact with. I will remain by the Oracle and scan your results as they come in. When she is located, I will recall all of you, but until then let none of us rest."

Once again the population cheered, "Yea, yea." The Winged Locust People were the first to leave. Following their group leader, they flew by the king in a salute, then went out into the night to search.

And so it was with the Woolly Bees, the Lightning Pixies, and the Flying Horsemen. Next the Royal Guard, mounted on air scooters, departed. All the rest of the population marched by the king, saluted, and went out into the night. Soon the only ones who remained in the Great Hall were King Benjamin, Willard, and Boo.

Boo flew to the stand in front of the little king and asked, "Your Majesty, may I go out and look also?"

"No, replied the king, I have a special assignment for you."

The three returned to the Inner Chamber to watch the Oracle as all searching groups reported in. Upon returning to the Inner Chamber, Willard brought King Benjamin a tall stool to sit on in front of the Oracle. The king watched the various bands of searching commandos comb the countryside in search of Amanda.

Boo lighted beside King Benjamin and asked, "Wh-what special assignment d-d-did you ha-have for m-me?"

The little king replied, "Just outside the eastern border of our kingdom, by the hanging bluffs, you will find an adobe house. A very elderly and wise Chinese gentleman by the name of Danny Wo lives there. As humans go, he is very gifted in the art of extrasensory perception and visions. His talents and gifts have been passed down to him for many generations.

"Long before your time, Boo, Danny Wo was in this chamber. He and his ancestors before him are the only other human beings besides the boy, Kevin, and his family to know our secrets. Danny Wo, like his family before him, is a very good and longtime friend of our people. I may need his special gifts to find Amanda. Boo, I wish for you to fly there and request that Danny Wo come here."

"Shall I w-w-wait and return with him?"

"No," replied the king, "Danny Wo will only travel on his old donkey and it will take him half a day to get here." Boo excused himself from the king's presence and flew away on his mission.

As the night wore on, Willard watched the little king peer into the Oracle and pace about the room, then repeat the same process. At last Willard asked, "What will you do when she is located?"

"We will go after her, of course."

Willard approached King Benjamin and asked, "Have you considered the wisdom of that?"

"What do you mean, Willard?"

"Do you wish for me to explain in detail?" asked Willard.

"Yes." The king sat on a stool.

"Eons ago, when your ancestors built all the instruments

of power and knowledge, they designed them to function upon the Light of Good in their people. Acts of compassion, love, and unselfishness make the Light stronger in the people and our instruments serve us better. But any act of aggression or violence, except in self-defense, dims the Light in our people and weakens the instruments that serve us." King Benjamin listened as Willard continued his explanation. "Now, Your Majesty, what you have committed our people to do at this time is good and the Light is strong. But should we attempt a rescue and meet with resistance, it could erupt into violence and damage the Light in our people. Do you wish to risk that?"

King Benjamin leaped from the stool to pace around the Oracle while he considered Willard's statement. "Willard, what is your counsel on this matter?"

Willard replied, "Continue the search until you locate Amanda, then allow the animal and human families to carry out the rescue."

The king angrily shouted, "Do you mean we must stand idly by and do nothing?"

"We can counsel, plan and advise them, but we should not have our people get involved in any act of violence or aggression against the human or animal population of this world. It is an interrelationship problem between human and animal kingdoms of this planet and would best be handled by them."

King Benjamin hopped back upon the stool and peered into the Oracle. "I will consider carefully your counsel concerning our people's welfare."

As dawn broke, Boo returned from his visit to Danny Wo and informed the king that Danny would be there before noon.

It was almost midday in the Enchanted Valley when Danny Wo arrived and was admitted to the Inner Chamber.

No one knew how old this marvelous little Chinese soothsayer was. He was small in size, and his eyes twinkled and glistened with wisdom and kindness. His smile was accented by a little white goatee. His graying hair was combed back and braided into a pigtail that hung to the middle of his shoul-

70

ders. A scarlet robe with emerald and yellow dragons painted on it covered him from his neck to his sparkling silver and gold sandals. At the top of his head sat a rounded green and red hat with a large crystal bobber on top.

He was greeted by King Benjamin, who said, "Thank you for coming. It has been a very long time, my old friend."

Danny Wo graciously bowed and replied, "I owe you much, Great One, how can I be of service?"

The king explained to Danny Wo all that had happened and asked him to use his special gifts and knowledge to help them locate Amanda. Danny agreed. He approached the Oracle and pulled three beautifully colored round crystal stones from his robe. One was red, one blue, and one green. He rolled them about in his hand as he studied the images being projected on the Oracle. After he had reviewed all that had transpired, he opened his hand and the three colored stones lit up and rose slowly until they were directly in front of his face. Then, moving rapidly in a circular motion around his head, they formed a brilliant aura as he told what he was seeing in a vision.

"The one you seek," intoned Danny Wo, "was taken captive by a ruthless human, who is called Hunter John. He has captured other small animals and, along with Amanda, has leased them to a scientific institution doing research in animal behavior. They are to be returned to Hunter John upon completion of the experimentation. Then he plans to slay them and sell their fur. I see her there now. She is in a small cage that is surrounded by many other cages, all of which are full of various animals."

The colored stones once again regrouped in front of his face and sank into Danny Wo's hand. He turned to the king and said, "Great One, you will find the one you seek in a scientific institution for the study of animal behavior in Dallas."

King Benjamin rushed to the Oracle and instructed all who were searching to concentrate their efforts on the Dallas area.

As the afternoon passed slowly, King Benjamin paced the floor and waited. It was nearly midafternoon when Sammy, the group leader of the Woolly Bees, reported the anxiously awaited news. Summoning the king to the Oracle, Sammy informed him, "Your Majesty, we have found Amanda. She is well and in good spirits." The king tossed his tiny crown into the air and, as tired as he was, leaped for joy.

Sammy then related to the king some very tragic information. "Your Majesty, the experiments are over. All the furry animals are to be returned to Hunter John. He is coming for them this afternoon. He is going to take them to his farm, and tomorrow he intends to skin them and sell their furs."

A silence fell over the Chamber. It was broken by King Benjamin, who jumped onto his Oracle and vowed, "That black-hearted son of a slime ball! I-I'll have him skinned and his carcass hung out in the sun to rot!" Then, looking at Willard, who was shaking his head, the little king angrily retorted, "All right, Willard, I won't do that, but we must plan a rescue quickly."

Leaping back on his stool, the king, looking into the Oracle at Sammy, the leader of the Woolly Bees, instructed, "Keep a few of your best flyers with you and stay close to Amanda. Keep me posted on all movements and send the rest of your flyers home." Using the Oracle, he contacted all search parties and told them Amanda had been found. Thanking them for their magnificent efforts, he instructed them to return immediately.

Boo, horrified at the thought of Rowdy's mother being skinned, flew down beside King Benjamin and said, "Your Majesty, I-I am of this world, and I-I am n-not b-bound by your laws. I-I want to find this Hunter J-John and puncture his neck!"

The king looked at him and said, "Don't tempt me, Boo. Besides, he is so evil, his blood would probably poison you!"

Danny Wo stepped forward and said, "My debt to you is great. I would be honored to help any way I can in this noble effort."

King Benjamin had been without rest for two days and nights. He was very weary from watching the Oracle and co-ordinating the search efforts. "You have already been of great assistance and I would not trouble you further, except that I have less than twenty-four hours to save her. You are a part of this world and not bound by our laws, so yes, my friend, there is a way you can help. First you must agree to being shrunk, temporarily, to our size."

"If this is necessary, I agree."

King Benjamin said, "Willard, take Danny to the Chamber of Reduction and set the instruments for the reduction to last only twenty-four hours." Then he turned to Danny and Boo. "After Danny is reduced in size, I want the two of you to take our fastest air scooter and fly to Hunter John's farm and map out the entire area for me." The king handed Danny Wo a small box. "This device will allow you to transmit all your information back to me. Then, my friends, go to the old farm and tell the children all we know. Have them get Sebastian, Sassy, and Rowdy, then all of you meet me at Fangs' cave at midnight. There we will finalize plans to rescue Amanda."

King Benjamin noticed a troubled look on Danny Wo's face. "Are you afraid of being reduced in size?"

"No," replied Danny Wo, "I know it will last but a short time, but I am concerned about our method of travel. I have never traveled on anything faster than my faithful old donkey

and now, Your Majesty, you wish to whisk me through the air at tremendous speeds atop a small piece of metal? That is what troubles me."

King Benjamin answered, "Danny, my precious friend, we have less than twenty-four hours to save Amanda and the other furry animals. It would take you at least two days to travel there on your donkey. Let me assure you, Boo is well-experienced in flying the air scooters. You will be safe."

"I am sure all will be well," Danny Wo said as he followed Willard to the Chamber of Reduction.

In a few moments Willard returned, carrying the tiny Chinese man in his hand. An air scooter was brought to the entrance of the magnesium tree. Boo and the nervous Danny Wo climbed on and zoomed toward Hunter John's farm. The king chuckled as he watched the frightened Danny Wo hanging tightly to Boo. Danny's pigtail stood straight out in the wind.

Chapter 11

Preparing for Rescue

The fluffy white Texas clouds slowly tinted orange as the sun set in the west and the shadows of darkness slipped in quietly. King Benjamin was informed that Hunter John had picked up Amanda and the other furry animals and was returning to his farm with them.

Boo and Danny Wo arrived at Hunter John's farm. As they circled the farm, Danny Wo used the small box that King Benjamin gave him and sent pictures of the area back to the Enchanted Kingdom for King Benjamin and his advisors to study.

Boo guided the air scooter inside the huge barn that was filled with holding cages. The cages lined two walls of the barn and were stacked four high, giving the gloomy appearance of a prison. Some of the cages already contained animals that had been trapped in the region north and west of the Big Thicket. Boo brought the air scooter to rest in the center of the barn. Then he flew from cage to cage, talking to the animals, telling them to remain quiet. He told them that they would be set free sometime in the night. Danny Wo moved about on the ground as quickly as his tiny legs could carry him, studying the locked cage doors.

As the last of daylight faded, Danny stood at one end of the barn with his back to the setting sun. He scanned the huge barn with the small box, sending vital pictures to the Enchanted Kingdom. Suddenly he noticed a large, eerie shadow coming over him and turned to see the horrifying sight of Spike's evil eyes glaring down at him. Standing beside this shrewd and vicious black Doberman was the equally terrifying sight of Otis, the clumsy and not so bright brown chow dog.

Spike's lips curled up on the side of his tremendous jaws, showing his deadly, sharp teeth. He said to Otis, "It's supper time, Otis. How about a little Chinese food?"

Otis tilted his head to one side and looked down at Danny with his big, round, dumb eyes and replied, "Oh, yes, Chinese food is my favorite. Can I have the drumsticks?"

"Otis, you idiot, drumsticks come on chickens and turkeys!"

Boo had seen the danger that Danny was in and dived straight into Spike's face. He slapped the dog with his wings, distracting him, and yelled, "Run for cover!"

While Spike snapped at Boo, Danny scurried across the open floor toward the safety of some empty crates.

Spike lunged after him, and just as it seemed Danny was doomed to be caught in Spike's deadly jaws, Otis came bounding in from the side, yelling, "I got him, Spike!" The two dogs collided at full speed, allowing Danny to reach the safety of the crates.

While the dogs rolled and tumbled in their collison, Boo mounted the air scooter and quickly picked up Danny. They made their escape flying past the dogs, who were still getting untangled. Spike was very angry at Otis' bungling. He was biting poor old Otis about the neck and ears and shouting at him, "Otis, you fool! I don't know why the master keeps you!"

Danny and Boo flew out the barn door and headed toward the children's farm. It was well after dark when they arrived at the old farmhouse. Uncle Jim was away overnight at a convention. Pete was caring for the children. Tommy, Kevin, and Donna were watching television in the living room, while Pete washed the evening meal dishes.

Boo and Danny Wo slowly circled the house, stopping in front of the windows as they passed them, looking for the children. They stopped at the kitchen window and came face to face with Pete.

Pete dropped a plate as he gazed at them. "It's happenin' again!" He rushed into the living room, his face pale, and said, "I believe old Pete needs you to reassure him he is okay again."

"Why?" asked Donna.

"Well, Missy Donna," said Pete, "in the kitchen window there is a teeny Chinaman and a little cross-eyed bat lookin' in and grinnin' at old Pete."

"That's got to be Boo!" exclaimed Tommy.

"Who is Boo?" asked Pete. He followed the children back into the kitchen, but they saw nothing at the window.

Kevin replied, "It is too lengthy to explain now, Pete." The children dashed upstairs to their bedroom and opened the window to await Boo. Soon, drifting slowly on the air scooter through the open window, came Boo and Danny Wo.

Pete had followed the children upstairs and was standing,

77

holding his hands clasped on top of his head, in the doorway as he watched Boo bring the air scooter to a gentle rest on the bed where the children were sitting.

Kevin said, "Hi, Boo! What brings you here and who is your friend?"

Boo introduced Danny Wo and then related to them all the events concerning Amanda's proposed rescue. The children were overjoyed about helping in the rescue of Sassy and Rowdy's mother and agreed to be at Fangs' cave at midnight.

"However," added Kevin, "we do have one problem." He pointed to Pete, who was still standing in the doorway, extremely confused.

Pete stepped forward and asked, "Little Kevin, why is it that I can hear you say something to the little bat, then you wait, then you speak again as though the little bat had said something to you? Pete does not hear the little bat say anything to you. Please explain."

Danny Wo approached Kevin. "Honorable Kevin, will you permit your servant to answer?"

Kevin replied, "Yes."

Danny Wo faced Pete, bowed graciously, and said, "Honorable Pete, there are many mysteries in this life that are best left unexplained. I suggest you trust noble children and leave these tea leaves unturned."

Pete attempted to return Danny's respect by bowing, then said, "I think the little Chinaman is right. Old Pete doesn't believe he wants to know all, but you can count on me to help in any way."

"Very well," said Danny Wo, "just before midnight, a transport vehicle will arrive here to take you and the honorable children to a rendezvous point with others who are going to assist in this worthy cause." Pete and the children agreed they would be ready.

Boo then said to Kevin, "W-we must g-go now to the raccoons a-and prepare them." Danny Wo and Boo departed on the air scooter and flew to the old hickory to prepare the raccoons and other animals for the rescue.

Back in the Enchanted Kingdom, King Benjamin had summoned his captains and advisors once again to the Inner

Chamber. He instructed his captains to select twenty-five from among their best.

To his advisors he said, "Prepare five flying platforms and twenty air scooters for departure and have them brought to the Great Hall immediately." While his captains and advisors carried out their instructions, Willard and the king went over the plan to rescue Amanda. The king then told Willard, "I have given your advice, concerning the welfare of our people, careful consideration, and this plan will avoid any of our people being brought into a situation of confrontation with the human or animal populations. They will simply be a diversion to the hunter and his dogs and serve only in a pickup and transportation capacity. But, Willard, as for myself," continued the king, "I fully intend to be in the heat of the conflict if there is any. I will risk my own well-being to do what I believe is just."

Willard looked at the noble little king and said, "May the Light of Good burn bright in you."

King Benjamin departed for the Great Hall to take command of his valiant force. The king instructed one flying platform to go to the old farm for the children and rendezvous with him at Fangs' cave. Stepping on to the lead flying platform, he stood proudly and erectly as a captain would at the helm of his ship. Leading the other airships, the king flew out of the Great Hall into the night toward Fangs' cave.

Boo and Danny Wo arrived at the raccoons' old hickory and, awakening them from their sleep, told the raccoon family all that had happened. With tears of joy and excitement, Sebastian, Rowdy, and Sassy took turns dancing around hugging each other and then embracing Boo and Danny. Sebastian sent Sassy and Rowdy to summon some of their friends to assist them while he departed to gather other friends. They were all to meet at Fangs' cave at midnight.

While the raccoons hurried through the night, gathering their friends, the air platform arrived at the children's home. The children and dogs quickly scrambled on top, while Pete cautiously climbed aboard, tipping his hat at the curious looking Woolly Bee who was piloting the airship.

Pete said, "Good evening, Mister ah — Mister ah —

whatever you are, good evening to you anyway!" The air platform rose and moved quietly through the night toward Fangs'
cave.

Just after midnight the children arrived at the cave and
found King Benjamin with his forces and the raccoons and
their friends waiting for them. As the airship came to rest in
the middle of the wonderfully curious collection of animals
and beings from another world, everyone present could feel
the bonds of love and good that were uniting them in their
mission of mercy.

Sassy and Rowdy bounded over and leaped upon the
children, bubbling with joy and excitement. Sassy said, "Isn't
it wonderful! We're going to get Mama!"

Sheriff Dallas Possum was coordinating the animals. He
said, "Let all the animal population gather around the king's
flying platform so we may be instructed on each of our parts
in this rescue of Amanda and our other friends." All gathered
around to listen to King Benjamin's plan.

The king raised his right hand and said, "My friends,
may the Light of Good be with us tonight. Each of you has

come here and placed your own life in danger to help your fellow creatures. Such love and courage is touching to the heart." The king paused for a second, then continued, "Let me bring you up to date on what is happening. Sammy, the group leader of the Woolly Bees, has been staying close to Amanda. He has informed me that Hunter John has picked up Amanda and over one hundred other animals. The hunter has with him another human called Gory Gary."

At the mention of Gory Gary's name, a loud cry burst forth from the animals, "Oh, no!"

The king then continued, "He has been hired to assist in the slaughter of all the animals they are bringing with them, as well as the animals now in the hunter's barn. This is a total of over two hundred creatures. Now, what do you know about this Gory Gary?"

Arvin, one of the Armadillo brothers, spoke up, "He bein' the scourge of all that be bad. He sure enuff bein' evil and delights in the sufferin' of little critters."

The other brother, Marvin, added, "He bein' hunch backed with flarin', buggy eyes. He be havin' a nose that bein' longer than Arvin's and mine put together, with a big, ugly black wart on the side. His laugh bein' so wicked it be makin' your bones turn to powder."

Then added Arvin, "The evil animal skinner be havin' only one great fear. He bein' terrified of snakes."

"Somebody call me?" asked old Fangs. "Just let me at this evil one and I'll teach him some manners!"

Sheriff Possum spoke. "If Gory Gary has been hired, he will start killing our friends at sunrise." Sassy and Rowdy sat clutching tightly to Sebastian as they listened to the horrifying description of Gory Gary.

King Benjamin reassured them that none of the animals would be in captivity at sunrise. He explained his plan. "Four flying platforms and twenty air scooters will be circling the hunter's farm, while I fly one platform into the barn. Danny Wo and I must get the key that unlocks the cages while Hunter John sleeps. All of you will be divided into groups and my captains will teach each group what its assignment is. Once your assignment is complete, return and board one of

the circling platforms. Should any of you get in a dangerous spot, watch for one of the air scooters to move in and pick you up quickly." All the animals were now divided into groups and their assignments explained to them.

King Benjamin once again spoke. "I have just been informed by Sammy, the group leader of the Woolly Bees, that Hunter John has arrived at his farm. He has parked his truck in the barn with all the animals still in their cages on the truck. Sammy says that the hunter and Gory Gary have retired to the hunter's cabin, leaving Spike and Otis to watch. Now it is time, my friends. Please load onto the flying platform that has been assigned to you."

All of the courageous little creatures of the forest climbed aboard. The air platforms rose and, in a marvelous caravan, sailed by moonlight through the night air toward Hunter John's farm — and their destinies.

Chapter 12

The Rescue

The moon was half full, providing a soft, eerie light upon the open fields surrounding Hunter John's cabin and barn. As the rescue party arrived, a dim light burned in the hunter's cabin, while the inside of the barn was engulfed in darkness.

Pulling the nets brought by the Sagittarians from the flying platforms, the animals divided into their groups. Dragging their nets, they slowly made their way to assigned positions around the cabin and barn. Under the cover of the darkness they began putting their nets in place to trap Spike and Otis.

Pete proudly prepared for his assignment, which was to ride atop Gee and wait in the shadows of the trees. If needed, he would provide cover for the escaping animals.

Four of the flying platforms took their positions around the cabin and barn. Each platform was escorted by five air scooters. They began moving in a circle around the area, in the way that Indians rode in a circle around the wagon trains in the Old West.

Sammy, the group leader of the Woolly Bees, and his companions, who had been waiting with Amanda, flew out to greet the rescue party. Sammy approached King Benjamin and said, "Your Majesty, all the animals in the barn await you. The dogs, Spike and Otis, are sleeping between the cabin and barn. Hunter John has fallen asleep in his chair in the cabin and the key you need is in the hunter's shirt pocket. But Gory Gary is walking somewhere around the area."

King Benjamin thanked Sammy for staying with Amanda. The king then told Sammy and his companions to join the others on the flying platforms. The pilots were to keep moving slowly and stay close to the ground so as not to be seen.

Boo was piloting the air platform carrying the king, Danny, the raccoon family, the children and their dogs, old Fangs, and Lonesome Skunk. Boo quietly flew the airship into the barn. While all unloaded, King Benjamin instructed Boo to move the air platform a distance from the barn and wait for a signal to return and pick him up. Boo backed the airship out and brought it to rest in the shadow of a large oak tree about two hundred yards from the barn. There he waited for the signal to return.

The raccoon family's hearts beat fast with excitement as they began searching through the darkened barn for Amanda. Knowing that Gory Gary was somewhere about, they could not call out to her, so they began moving quietly from cage to cage, searching for her.

At last Sassy, crawling along one of the rails of the truck, came face to face with her mother. With tears running down and dropping off the end of her cute black nose, she placed her loving little fingers through the wire cage. Touching Amanda's face, she whispered softly, "I love you, Mama."

Amanda tenderly kissed Sassy's fingers and whispered back, "I love you too. I have missed you all so much . . . but be very quiet, Sassy, as that evil man is somewhere just outside the barn."

Sassy scurried quietly along the bed of the truck until she found Sebastian and Rowdy. She whispered to them where Amanda was and about Gory Gary being outside the barn.

While Sassy moved through the darkness to tell the others, Sebastian and Rowdy went to Amanda. Touching each other as best they could through the wire cage, they whispered

their feelings of love and joy. From behind Amanda in the darkness came a shy voice that said, "Hi, Rowdy." Peering past his mother's shoulder, Rowdy tried to see who was speaking to him.

Amanda softly said, "Come up here, child."

Moving from the corner of the cage into the moonlight that filtered through the cracks in the barn was a cute little girl raccoon. Her fur was splotched, brown and gray, and she was wearing overalls with many patches covering the tears and worn spots. "This is Sebastian and Rowdy," Amanda continued, "and this is Patches. She was orphaned when she was very small and had to take care of herself in the Big Woods just north of our forest. She was carted up at the same time I was and was sent to the institution."

Rowdy gazed at Patches for a second with his mouth hanging open. Then, cocky and self-assured, he placed his hands on his hips and said to Patches, "Don't worry, kid, we'll have you out of here in a jiffy."

Their conversation was interrupted by the sound of Gory Gary approaching the barn, with his lantern squeaking as it swung in his hand. All present scurried quickly to hide behind some bales of hay as Gory Gary entered the barn. Walking through the barn, he checked the cages. Stopping in front of Amanda's cage, he held his lantern up and, with his evil, bulged eyes, peered in at Amanda and Patches. "My darlings, in the morning I shall part you from your furs. Then, in the afternoon, old Gory shall dine on raccoon pie baked with sweet potatoes." Rubbing his stomach, he laughed wickedly.

Rowdy, terrified and outraged, began climbing over the bales of hay to attack him but was pulled back by Sebastian. "Not now, son. Be patient."

Continuing to laugh, the evil one held his lantern high and shouted, "This day you are all mine and I shall have your hides!" Going out the barn door, laughing, he spotted Spike and Otis lying asleep between the barn and cabin. He kicked both dogs and shouted, "Wake up, you lazy devils, and earn your keep or I will skin you too!" Then, muttering, he walked to the cabin.

The little group sat huddled behind the hay, listening to Gory Gary's fading sounds. Suddenly, a small, squeaky voice from behind them said, "He's a mean one, ain't he?"

"Who's there?" asked Tommy.

"Just me," the voice replied.

"Well, come out where we can see you," said Kevin.

With that, a bodacious little mouse bounded up on the hay in front of them and said, "I'm Jodie. Are you going to spring all the animals tonight?"

"Yes," replied Sebastian.

"Need some more help?" asked Jodie.

"We are grateful for all the help we can get," said Sebastian.

"Well, I'm your boy! I know every inch of the cabin and barn. But how are you going to get the cages unlocked?"

Sebastian explained, "We must get the key from inside the hunter's cabin."

"Well," said Jodie, "you've got a problem."

"What kind of problem?" asked King Benjamin.

"Well," answered Jodie, "first you must get past the dogs — and you just heard the evil one wake them. You might slip around old, dumb Otis, but the shrewd Spike will be on you in a second and swallow you whole! Now, if you can get by the dogs you still have to get inside the cabin. The hunter always latches the door from the inside."

"Do you know a way in?" asked King Benjamin

"Yes," said Jodie, "I can get in through a crack in the floor and crawl along the window ledge and trip the latch on the door for you."

"Would you be so kind?" asked Sebastian.

"It will be a pleasure," replied Jodie, "but you must still get past the dogs."

"I have an idea. Leave them to me," stated Charles.

Sebastian, remembering how clever Charles was at setting Sassy and Rowdy free from Hunter John's trap, asked, "What is your plan, Charles?"

"Well, Samantha, come up here beside me a minute." Samantha leaped up beside him. Charles stroked Samantha's head with his paw. "Sam, you're a fine looking female and Spike and Otis are two healthy male dogs. I want you to go out there and use your feminine wiles to lure them off a distance."

Samantha's eyes widened as she shook with fear. "You mean, you want me to go out there alone and face those two brutes?"

Charles reassured her, saying, "Now, Sam, you can do it! Just flirt a little and then prance off. They will stumble all over each other following you."

"Well," asked the nervous Samantha, "what do I do when they follow me?"

"Just lead them into one of the net traps, then they will be out of the way. But be sure you give us enough time to free the animals first," said Charles.

Samantha agreed and pranced out the barn door. With a flirtatious walk she passed by Spike and Otis. Glancing over her shoulder, she said, "Hiya, big fellas!"

Otis started to get up, but Spike put his paw on Otis' head and pushed his face down into the dirt. "Keep your mouth shut, dummy. This is a job for a real dog! I'll take care of this matter myself."

The annoyed Otis pulled his nose out of the dirt and said, "I'm not going to stay behind while you have all the fun! I'm coming along too!" Samantha pranced away, with both dogs strutting after her.

Charles watched Samantha lure the two dogs away and told the others they could proceed to the cabin.

King Benjamin, Rowdy, and Danny Wo dashed through the darkness to the door of the cabin, while Jodie scurried under the cabin and up through the crack in the floor. Climbing the curtains to the window ledge, he worked his way to the edge and tripped the door latch.

Outside the door, some empty crates were stacked on top of each other. Rowdy bounded up to the top of them and, turning the door knob, pushed the door open just enough for them to slip inside.

Old Fangs had slithered across to the cabin, hoping, when the time came, to get an opportunity to put a good scare into Gory Gary. He climbed a small tree that grew by the steps to the porch, and there he waited for his chance.

Inside the cabin, Hunter John was still sleeping in his chair by the fireplace. Danny, Rowdy, and the king were quietly discussing how to get the key from the hunter's shirt pocket when Jodie said, "No problem . . . watch this!" The daring little mouse dashed across the floor and up Hunter John's leg. Bouncing across his lap and up to his shirt pocket, Jodie reached in, pulled out the key, and waved it at the others. Then he bounded back to the floor, leaving the hunter undisturbed. He hurried across to King Benjamin and presented him with the key.

"Well," whispered the king, "you're quite a gutsy little fellow."

"That's me, gutsy all the way!" agreed Jodie.

King Benjamin gave the key to Danny. "Take this to the children and have them free all the animals. Then signal Boo to bring the air platform back to the barn. See that the children and all the slower critters are loaded onto the platform. Prepare all the rest of them to make a run for the safety of the other platforms on my signal."

Danny slipped through the partially opened door and re-

turned to the barn to carry out his instructions.

King Benjamin then sidled up to Rowdy and whispered, "How about a good prank on Hunter John?"

Rowdy's eyes lit up and he asked, "What did you have in mind?"

The king said, "Follow me." Leaving Jodie to watch the door, the two of them slipped quietly across the floor to Hunter John's chair. Pointing to the sleeping hunter's shoelaces, the king said, "Shall we?"

With an amusing, devilish grin, Rowdy replied, "Allow me!"

The two cautiously tied the hunter's shoelaces together while he slept soundly in his chair.

Just as they finished their mischievous task, they heard Gory Gary approach the cabin. Rowdy and the good king tried to make it out the door but saw that Gary was too close. They quickly hid under a stool by the door.

Gory Gary saw the door standing partially open, then he noticed that the dogs were gone. Pulling his long knife out, he muttered, "Something is not right." He shouted for the dogs to return just as Samantha was about to lead them into a net trap.

Spike fumed, "Wouldn't you know it? That worthless human is determined to spoil our fun!" Then, looking at Samantha, he said, "Gorgeous, you wait right here. Your Big Daddy'll be back in just a minute!"

Spike and Otis ran toward the cabin as Samantha made a dash for the barn. When she arrived at the barn, the children had just finished freeing all the animals. Sebastian and Sassy were embracing Amanda.

Boo had been signaled and was gliding the air platform back into the barn. The children and slower animals began loading, while the swifter animals gathered about the door preparing to make a run for the safety of the circling platforms.

Back at the cabin, Gary scolded Spike and Otis for leaving and ordered them to lie on the porch by the cabin door. He pushed the door open and approached the sleeping hunter. "You'd better wake up, John. Something is not right."

Hunter John yawned and said, "Don't worry, Gary, the animals are locked in their cages and I have the key right here in my pocket." A look of despair came over the hunter's face as he felt the empty shirt pocket. Leaping to his feet, he shouted, "Quick, to the barn!" But when he started to run, his tied shoelaces tripped him. He fell across a small table, knocking Gory Gary to the floor with him.

As the evil one rolled across the floor, he saw the king, Rowdy, and Jodie hiding under the stool. "So you are the little devils who are trying to rob old Gary! I'll cut your gizzards out!"

King Benjamin shouted, "Boys, let's make a run for it!" Out the open door they ran, leaping over Spike and bouncing off Otis' nose.

"Ouch, ouch, ouch," yipped Otis as each of them used his nose for a springboard.

The three little comrades were making their wild dash toward the barn as Gory Gary came charging out the door, flashing his knife. He yelled after them, "You are going to be fish bait when old Gary gets through carving you up!" Spike

and Otis, stunned for a second, leaped to their feet and became entangled in Gory Gary's legs as they attempted to pursue. Tangled up with each other, all three toppled off the porch and rolled and tumbled on the ground.

Gory Gary kicked at the dogs, shouting, "Get away from me, you morons!" After getting untangled Spike and Otis lunged after the king, Rowdy, and Jodie.

Gory Gary pulled himself up by the tree where old Fangs was hanging. This was the opportunity old Fangs had been hoping for. He slithered out on the limb directly over Gary, who was picking up his knife. Fangs dropped from the limb and fell about Gory Gary's neck. He curled himself around and, looking the evil Gary straight in the eyes, flashed his wooden fangs and hissed, "Want to hang around together for a while?"

The terrified Gary began screaming and running backwards, trying to shake and slap the old snake off him. After a few seconds of absolute terror and screaming, he managed to get free of the snake and ran toward the barn.

Old Fangs was lying on his back, kicking his tail in the air, laughing in sheer delight as he called after evil Gary. "Leaving so soon, Mr. Gory?"

Meanwhile, back at the barn, Lonesome Skunk was watching the king, Rowdy, and Jodie run toward the barn with Spike and Otis gaining on them. Lonesome dashed out to meet them. As they passed each other, he shouted, "Now it's my turn to help!" Lonesome spun around with his backside facing the oncoming dogs, popped his tail up, and drew aim. In a squirty flash he scored a direct hit in Otis' face.

Temporarily half-blinded by the skunk juice, Otis turned around and around. Spike stopped quickly to avoid running into Otis, who was totally covered with skunk juice and had lost his sense of direction. Spike began running in the other direction to get out of Otis' way. Upon seeing Spike run, Otis chased after, believing that Spike was pursuing the animals. Now, this was quite a humorous sight to behold: Spike frantically running away to avoid the smelly Otis, and Otis frantically running after Spike because he didn't know what else to do.

Suddenly, *zip, slap*, both dogs were bagged tightly in a net trap. Helplessly bound up together, Spike attempted to push the foul-smelling Otis away, saying, "Why must my life be afflicted with fools and idiots!"

As the animals that sprung the net trap left, they heard Otis reply, "I don't know!"

Rowdy, King Benjamin, and Jodie had reached the barn and leaped upon the loaded platform. The king gave the order for all the other animals to run for the safety of the circling airships. Out the barn door they all dashed, while King Benjamin piloted the flying platform out behind them.

Gory Gary had reached the barn and grabbed hold of the side of the platform as it sailed out the door. As he attempted to pull himself up, Rowdy ran over. By biting and pushing on him, he succeeded in making the evil one lose his grip and fall. But Rowdy also toppled over the side onto the ground.

Gory Gary, flashing his long knife, ran after Rowdy, saying, "At least I will get you!"

Boo had seen Rowdy fall and flew back to help him. Boo flew into the face of Gory Gary again and again, attempting to divert him from Rowdy. Then, in a horrible motion, the evil Gary's knife slashed Boo. The wounded Boo fluttered to the ground, unconscious.

Rowdy raced to Boo's side and made his stand against Gory Gary. Rowdy bared his teeth, snarling and growling, as the evil Gary approached them.

Laughing wickedly, Gary said, "The two of you will not see the sun rise."

It seemed the two little critters were doomed as Gory Gary lifted the knife up to make the fatal slash. But out of the darkness two adult raccoons leaped through the air, landing in the middle of the evil one's chest and knocking the knife from his hand, causing him to stumble backwards. The evil one caught his balance, pulled Sebastian and Amanda loose, and threw them through the air. Turning to look for his knife, he saw it lying against a large stone. As the evil Gary bent to pick it up, he felt a sudden burst of heat singeing his clothes. Turning quickly, he saw the terrifying sight of Gee leaping toward him, breathing flames. Screaming in terror, Gary ran for the cabin.

Close behind was Pete riding on Gee, waving his hat in the air and shouting, "You like a little heat to warm yourself with, animal skinner?" Then he shouted to Gee, "Give him another snort!" With each command a burst of flame shot out and struck close to the fleeing, terrorized animal skinner.

The air scooters dashed about the open field, plucking up the running animals and dropping them to the safety of the closest flying platform.

In the meantime, Hunter John had managed to get his shoes untied and was watching the events from the porch. He saw Gory Gary running for the cabin with Gee close behind, breathing fire.

At this point, fear overcame anger and greed. The hunter decided to give it up. He went back inside his cabin and locked the door behind him.

The evil Gary saw he could not make it to the cabin before Gee overtook him, so he leaped into the open well to escape Gee's hot breath.

Pete rode up beside the open well and shouted down to him, "How do you like them apples, Evil Gary?" As Pete rode away he said, "You mess with our friends, the animals, again and we will be back!"

King Benjamin had returned to Boo's side. As Rowdy helped load Boo's unconscious body onto the air platform, he remembered Willard's words at their first meeting, "Do not judge Boo too harshly, as he can and will become a good and loyal friend."

All, at last, were loaded onto the flying platforms, leaving behind two disturbed dogs, one confused hunter, and a wet Gory Gary.

As they sailed away, they saw Gary climb out of the well, shake his fist at them, and swear, "I will have my revenge upon you!"

While one of the Winged Locust People piloted their air platform, King Benjamin, Rowdy, Sassy, and the children all sat around Boo, who was still unconscious. Rowdy asked, "Will he be all right?"

King Benjamin put his arm around Rowdy and said, "Do not fear, his wound is not serious. I promise you, Rowdy, he will recover. And the two of you may taunt each other many times in the days to come."

Chapter 13

The King's Farewell Address

The sun was about to rise as the caravan arrived back at Fangs' cave. There it was met by a high-speed air vehicle that picked Boo up and whisked him away to the Enchanted Kingdom for treatment. There was a short period of jubilation as the animals hugged each other and talked about the experience of the night.

Then King Benjamin gathered the children and raccoons around him and said, "This has been an extraordinary experience."

Sebastian approached the king with gratitude and humility and said, "My family is together and safe because of you and your people. How can we ever repay you?"

Sassy and Rowdy placed their arms around the king as their tears dropped on his shoulders. "We love you too."

With his own eyes watering, King Benjamin looked up at Sebastian and replied, "In all the universe there is no greater payment than this." Then, stepping upon his platform, he asked to address all who were present. As all gathered round, he spoke. "My friends, it has been a choice privilege to be a part of this joyous reunion. I know that in your hearts tonight you wonder why there must be conflict between the animal and human population. The only answer I have for you is to be patient. Give the human population time to grow. I want you to know that we came from a world that had learned to live in peace with all around us as the Creator of all things in this universe intended. You see among you three human children who have learned to care and understand, and there are many more humans out there who have learned to live in peace with all. And so, my friends, in time all the human population will grow and come to understand this and there will be a day of great joy on this planet when all hurt ends. Then you will all be able to talk with all humans as you now can with these choice children.

"Now, my friends, I must bid you a fond farewell and return to my kingdom." The animal population cheered the noble little king as he stepped down. He approached the children and raccoons and said, "Now I must sadden you a little by telling you it is time for Gee to return with me. The evil Gary and Hunter John have seen him and will, for the lure of money, come hunting for him."

The children and raccoons were saddened, but realized it had to be. Pete hugged Gee and sobbed, "It was great sport you and I had tonight. Maybe someday I will see you again." Pete could not hear Gee's return compliment, but understood Gee's approval by the way he rubbed his nose against the side of Pete's head.

King Benjamin instructed one flying platform to stay behind and return the children to their home. Then, addressing the children one final time, he said, "Tommy, Kevin, Donna, the Light of Good burns brightly inside of you. Your hearts and minds have grown with understanding, kindness, and love to a point where your minds have the ability to communicate with all forms of life. You may keep the ring to contact me if necessary, but you no longer need it to talk with and understand the animals. You see, my wonderful little friends, all humans have this ability within them if they use unselfishness, understanding, love, and kindness in their lives. If they do, the Light of Good can grow until they put aside all prejudice and live at peace with all things. But, unfortunately, most humans choose the course of selfishness, greed, and igno-

rance. These things slowly destroy the Light of Good in them and they lose all understanding of things around them.

"Now, my youthful friends, remember this well. Good is more powerful than evil. And good will lead your lives into happiness. Do not give in to hate, selfishness, bigotry, or ignorance. These will destroy the Light of Good and you will lose your ability to comprehend all things about you."

Turning to Rowdy, the king said, "By the trunk of the old hickory you will find one air scooter. See that you use it wisely and upon your next visit to my kingdom I shall expect you to bring my marbles." King Benjamin joined Danny Wo on the lead platform. He looked around at all his new friends. The good king remarked to Danny Wo, "One so rich in the love of good friends can never be poor." As his airship sailed away, all waved a fond goodbye.

The children, Pete, and the dogs boarded their airship and, waving goodbye, sailed into the dawn toward home. All the animals began to return to their homes, leaving the raccoon family embracing each other.

Old Fangs looked at Jodie, who had no place to go, and

said, "Do you want to move into my cave with me?"

Jodie asked, "You won't eat me someday for lunch, will you?"

"Oh, no," said Fangs, "I made a promise to mend my ways and I intend to keep it. I'm strictly a vegetarian now."

"Well," said Jodie, "you got a roommate."

Sebastian and Amanda were about to depart with Sassy and Rowdy. They all noticed Patches, quietly standing alone in the dawn's early shadows, as she watched all the families leave. Together Sassy and Rowdy asked, "Papa, Mama, can we — ?"

Amanda interrupted them, "Say no more . . . of course we can." The entire raccoon family approached the sobbing Patches and stretched forth their arms. Amanda implored, "Patches, will you come join our family and let us be a part of your life?"

In a burst of joyful tears, Patches rushed into their arms. Great was this family's love and joy, and their hearts grew exceedingly on that beautiful spring morning.

Chapter 14

Return To Home

As the sun slowly climbed into the morning sky, King Benjamin arrived back at the Enchanted Kingdom. There he found Boo up hopping around, complaining about missing the final battle. Boo quickly asked if the raccoons and children were safe. King Benjamin reassured him all had returned safely.

Danny Wo shook his head sadly and said, "Your Majesty, Honorable Boo, I do not believe this conflict is over."

"Yes," replied the king, "I, too, believe we have not heard the last of the animal skinner, Gory Gary."

Willard asked, "Your Majesty, do you believe he will attempt to harm the children or animals?"

The king answered, "I do not believe he was aware of the children's presence, but he saw me, Pete, Danny, and Gee. There is so much hate, evil and greed in this man that I am certain he will not rest until he has made an attempt to track us down. Willard, I want you to tighten security in the Enchanted Kingdom and assign scouts to watch Gory Gary's movements. Boo, you must take care of your wounds. I am sure you will be needed to assist the animals very soon."

King Benjamin thanked Danny Wo for his assistance.

Danny was starting to regain his normal size as the reduction effects wore off.

Danny graciously dismissed himself from the king's presence, saying, "Noble One, I must prepare to return to my home, but should you need my services again, please do not hesitate to send for me."

Back at the farm, the children prepared for a nap after their long night of adventure. As they settled into their beds and slipped peacefully to sleep, they were unaware of the evil that Gary was planning.

Pacing Hunter John's cabin floor, Gory Gary said to the hunter, "John, I want those animals back. But more important, did you see that giant thing leaping across the field throwing flames? And that fat little king? There was also a tiny Chinese man." Stopping for a moment, he placed his hand under his jaw and bounced his fingers off his evil lips, then continued, "The monster, the little king, and the small Chinaman would be worth a fortune to us." Walking over, he gazed out the cabin window. His eyes squinted and twisted with an evil glare. "I will hunt them down. I will capture the monster and sell him and I will stuff the little king and Chinaman and display them on my fireplace mantel. When I have done that, and destroyed the raccoons, my revenge will be sweet!" he chuckled wickedly.

The raccoon family had returned to the old hickory. Rowdy prepared a hiding place next to the old tree for his air scooter, while Sassy helped Patches prepare a room for herself.

Sebastian and Amanda lovingly watched the young raccoons going about their tasks. Amanda looked at Sebastian. "Our family is truly blessed with love, understanding, and goodness."

Sebastian sighed. "Yes, all is well in our home again."

It was midmorning in the forest and it seemed for the moment that all was well. The wind gently blew through the trees and hummed a tune of peace on earth, goodwill toward all.

From the Author

Sassy & Rowdy express the good and fun-loving nature that is in so many of our hearts.

We hope you have enjoyed reading this adventure of Sassy & Rowdy, and that you are looking forward to reading all their books.

We welcome your comments on this book and would like to extend an invitation to the young and young at heart to submit your ideas on adventures for Sassy & Rowdy.

Address your letters to Sassy & Rowdy at P.O. Box 1883, Denton, Texas 76202.

Now Available